Seduced By A Billionaire

Erica Frost

Published by Erica Frost, 2022.

This is a work of fiction. Similarities to real people, places, or events are entirely coincidental.

SEDUCED BY A BILLIONAIRE

First edition. November 23, 2022.

Copyright © 2022 Erica Frost.

ISBN: 979-8223091929

Written by Erica Frost.

Table of Contents

Seduced By A Billionaire

By: Erica Frost

Foreword

Am I just going from one abusive relationship to another? Can a billionaire save me?

I was stuck working in a massage parlor. It was about the only job I could get, and my boyfriend Mark hated it. We were in the big city, supposedly living in the prime of our lives, but we argued all the time and he showed his love for me by hitting me.

I'd been lost in the foster system for years so I didn't know any better. I thought it was better to be hurt than to be alone. I wish I had someone to turn to, someone to help guide me.

Then Jack came along. He didn't think much of me at first either. What would a billionaire want with a girl like me? But I guess it's true what they say; opposites attract and boy did we attract in a BIG way.

Seduced By A Billionaire

Chapter One

"Why did you agree to work today? You knew I wanted to spend some time with you. I can't believe you Sandi, you always say that you want to spend more time together and then you go and do something like this! I had a nice day planned. It was going to be a surprise. Come on, can't you call them and cancel?"

Mark had an imploring look in his eyes. He was always so good with his squirming words at getting underneath my heart. He reached out towards me and seemed genuinely hurt. I hated doing this to him because it was true, I had asked him to be more attentive and less focused on having a good time with his buddies, but it shouldn't have been like this. I mean, this was my job!

"I appreciate that you've gone to a lot of trouble Mark, and I'm sorry, but I already made a commitment. Cindy wanted to swap shifts because it's her Mom's birthday. I didn't know you had anything planned."

"It was supposed to be a surprise," he said bitterly.

"Look, I'm only going to be gone during the day. We can still make a nice night of it," I said, moving closer towards him, swaying my hips slightly in the manner I knew he always liked. I fluttered my eyelashes and smiled coyly, trying to get him to see me as I always wanted him to see me. But he growled and he became this wild animal again. It was like something was coiled up inside him and it burst out when he got angry.

And Mark was always angry.

He moved with impossible speed and grabbed my forearm just above my wrist, digging his fingers in. Pain flared and tears welled up in my eyes. My body crumpled as I gazed into his merciless face.

"You shouldn't even be working there at all," he snarled, glaring at me with stormy eyes, his teeth bared like a wolf. "I've told you time and time again that I hate you working there. When are you going to quit?

God, the thought of you spending all day massaging other men makes me sick. It's not right. You might as well be a whore," he spat. It wasn't the first time we had had this argument and I doubted it would be the last. I'd long given up on trying to reason with him. His opinion was set in his mind like stone and there was nothing that was going to change it.

"I've been looking, you know I have!" I cried, begging him silently to relinquish his grip on me. Being strong was effortless for him. His muscles looked as though they had been hewn from rock, and there was nothing I could do to fight back against him. I had tried, oh yes, I had tried, but it only made him angrier. The best way was to placate him and remind him that I cared deeply for him, because I did care. Few others understood our relationship. Cindy, for example, told me that I should get out of there before permanent damage was done, but I was never in danger of that. Mark just needed to let off steam, that was all. She made it sound easy as well, as though finding someone to love you was just that simple. I knew it wasn't. I'd bounced around the foster system long enough to know that people didn't care easily. They would happily pass you around, and I was tired of being alone. Mark might not have been perfect, but at least he stuck around.

"If there was something else I could do then I would, but we need the money," I said. Mark let go of my arm. I withdrew it and cradled it like a baby bird, caressing the burning pain away. Mark swiped his hand through the air.

"I still don't like it. My friends all make jokes about it, you know? They keep asking me if they can get a discount because they're my buddies. It makes me a laughing stock and I hate being a laughing stock. Is that what you want? You have to find a way out of there quickly, because I'm tired of being the butt of a joke."

"I don't want that. You know I don't," I said meekly, my gaze flicking towards him for fear that he was going to lash out at me again.

Sometimes I don't know what's worse, his fists or his tongue. Either way the pain eventually fades away, but one cuts deeper than the other.

"You'd better get on with you then. If you're going to go you don't want to be late. I'll just keep myself occupied somehow, but don't you throw this back in my face. I don't want to hear you complain about me being a bad boyfriend again, because you're lucky to be with someone who is so understanding. Christ, you think anyone else would be happy to have you, knowing where you work?" he shook his head with shame.

"Thank you Mark," I whimpered, dragging myself away to get dressed for work. I was glad that my top was long sleeved so it could hide the marks. The last thing I needed was people asking about me, as though I was prey being hunted. It wasn't like that. Mark just had his quirks, that's all. Every relationship had trouble behind closed doors and we were no different. Besides, he was right. All my life I'd been taught that people didn't want me. Even when I was a button nosed girl people passed me by. First they said I was too young, then I was too old. Eventually you're in the foster system for so long that people start believing there's something wrong with you. Maybe they were right.

Mark was the first guy who actually showed he wanted me. I still remember the intensity with which he looked at me the first night we met. I was scared, but it was the good kind of scared, the kind that left tingles running all up and down my flesh, the kind that told me my life was never going to be the same again. Of course it wasn't perfect; no relationship ever was, but Mark stuck by me, so I was going to stick by him. Every relationship took sacrifices and a little pain was just the sacrifice that I needed to make.

I felt bad for disappointing him, because when he put his effort into something he really did try his best, and he wasn't wrong when he said that I had been begging him to make a little more effort. I was beginning to think I was asking too much. I always had these ideas of what a relationship should be like and sometimes I let myself get carried away. Not everything could be like in the movies though, although I wish it could have been.

I changed into my work clothes and then walked back out, kissing him on the cheek. Mark made a point to not turn his head and meet my lips with his. I said goodbye and left him to his TV show. He'd likely spend the day at the gym or with his buddies now. I was sure that he'd find a way to keep himself occupied, but my heart was filled with guilt that I had ruined the special day he had planned. Hopefully, by the time I returned he would cool off though. Mark's temper was either like fire or ice, and I wasn't sure which one I preferred. The dull ache in my wrist reminded me of the times he had unleashed himself in an inferno. Rage always had a way of taking him over, as though he was possessed by some other being. It churned and burst from him like a cyclone, primal energy that had nowhere else to go. Other times he was quiet, simmering underneath, each word cutting deeper into my soul until he reached the very heart of me.

I suppose I preferred the first.

I walked down the sidewalk. The air was crisp, and also hazy with the smog that lingered in a miasma. Cars surged by, leaving behind them a trail of thick smoke. Windows were boarded up with cardboard. Graffiti stained the walls. The road was pockmarked with potholes. In the distance I could see the rising, towering skyscrapers that gleamed as they touched the sun. Breath caught in my throat with awe as I gazed at them. It was as though they were a part of another world, as though I was just a mortal gazing up at the home of the gods. It was a sign that there was a better world out there, a better place, but it wasn't meant for someone like me.

I was destined to be here, in the gutters, with the rest of the rats. The world was a cruel place for us. We could see the shining towers and could feel the temptation of hope, but if it ever touched our hearts it would be a curse. I used to dream of something better, of a shining knight coming to rescue me as though I was some forgotten princess, but as time moved on I realized that I was just being stupid. Nobody was coming to rescue me because I was worthless. But at least I had Mark.

As I passed a homeless person on the street I pulled a crumpled note out of my pocket and handed it to them, figuring it was the least I could do. She thanked me profusely. For her this single dollar was a lifeline, and I knew that it wasn't the money she appreciated so much as just the recognition that she existed. It was so easy to see these people like ghosts and look through them rather than at them. But that's what people did; they just ignored their problems. She had yellow teeth and wore ragged, stained clothes. A torn up sleeping bag was rolled up beside her. Her hands were gnarled and arthritic. I doubted she was long for this world, and my heart sank as I knew that it could so easily have been me. If I didn't have Mark... God... I didn't know what I'd do.

*

I greeted Ally, who smiled at me and told me that my first client had arrived a little early and was already in the back waiting. It was just before midday, and I would work until about 7 before heading home. They weren't bad hours, and I was glad to have a little time to relax in the morning rather than having to drag myself out of bed at an unholy hour and feel like a ghoul. Ally was chipper as usual and we made a little chit chat as I hung up my coat and smoothed down my hair. Ally owned the salon. She was a white woman with platinum hair and she always looked made up like a doll. She was a tiny thing, and yet if pushed she had a hell of a temper on her. Cindy and I joked that she was like a Mom to us, although it was less of a joke to me. I never wanted to disappoint her so I tried to do the best job that I could, even though Mark hated that I was here. I guess I could understand it. Mark was a traditional guy and it can't have been easy for him to know that I spent my days rubbing lotion into men's backs, but it was just a job. Still, I guess I wouldn't have been comfortable knowing that he spent his days with his hands flesh deep in naked women, not that my job was glamorous at all. The men who came to my salon were not athletes. They were usually overweight and hairy, and just looking for an oasis of bliss in the stress that was their lives. It was often fascinating to talk to them though. A lot of them complained about their families and their wives. I wondered if they really meant it or if they were just blowing off steam. I always wanted to tell them how lucky they were, but that would have been unprofessional.

I walked into the small massage parlor. Ally had already lit the candles so a lavender scent filled the air, and shadows flickered on the walls. I pressed a button on the iPod to play the relaxing music. The sound of plucked harp strings settled in the room, a gentle ambience to lull the client into a relaxed state of mind.

"Good morning; I'm Sandi and I'll be taking care of you today," I said as I squeezed some lotion into my hands and walked towards the table. The man was face down, his arms stretched out above his head. He had already draped a towel over the back of his legs, but his feet dangled at the end of the table. The first thing I noticed is that he wasn't like the other men who came in here. While they treated this place like a refuge from the rigors of their life, this man looked like a warrior. He looked as though he was in control of himself. His back was a rippling expanse of defined muscles. His body was lean, yet powerful, and he exuded this aura as though he was casting a spell on me.

"I'm Jack," he said, his words muffled from below the table. A thick mane of hair, immaculately cut and styled, rested on his scalp. More dark hair flowed down his powerful forearms and legs. As soon as I touched his flesh I felt fire rush up my arms. This had never happened before, and I wondered what kind of man he was to have this effect on me, and then I immediately felt guilty, afraid that Mark would be able to sense these feelings playing on my mind. I cringed as my forearm cried out in pain. The last time he thought I'd been attracted to another man hadn't ended at all well for me. I shuddered as the echoes of pain swept through me, as his insults rained down like shards of glass. I closed my eyes to stem the flow of tears as I pressed down on this man's supple flesh. For the first time I felt guilty about my job.

Chapter Two

"So, is it normal to talk during these things?" Jack asked.

"You can do whatever like, whatever you find the most relaxing," I replied.

"I guess it wouldn't hurt to talk. I don't like silence. Never have. It just reminds me of an empty house," he said.

"I love it sometimes, but other times it can be hard," I said. Since I grew up in a foster care facility I rarely had privacy, and even when I was alone I could still hear the background noise of everyone living their lives. Silence was a rare commodity, and one that I cherished, although it wasn't always welcome. Sometimes the last thing I wanted was to be alone with my thoughts.

"I should have done this a long time ago," Jack groaned, his words creaking as I found a particularly tight knot in his back and plied it with my fingers, trying to loosen the tension.

"You are carrying a lot of tension, especially here, in your shoulders and the middle of your back. A lot of people don't realize how much tension they're carrying until they start to feel it ebb away."

"That's very true," he groaned, gasping a little.

"Is that too hard?" I checked, pausing for a moment. Jack shook his head, so I continued, using all my strength to massage the ache out of his muscles.

"So what do you do Jack?" I asked. There were a stock of questions I had at the ready for people who wanted to converse during the massage. Most of them didn't want to speak though, but I was always happy to pass the time. The trick was to not get too personal and to not touch on anything controversial.

"I manage people," he said.

"I can imagine how that would be stressful. People never do what you want them to," I said, laughing a little. He chuckled too.

"That is very accurate. I've always been meaning to get a massage, but it's so hard to find the time. But the tension just got too much and I told myself that I have to get down there. I've seen this place on my way to work and I don't know what it is, but there's something about it that has always caught my eye."

"I'm sure Ally will be pleased to hear that and of course you'll always be welcome again. Where do you work, in one of those tall skyscrapers?" I asked nonchalantly, assuming that he did given that most people passed by the salon on their way to work in the inner city.

"Yeah," Jack replied.

"It must be amazing to live there, to look out on the world around you and feel as though you're floating."

"Truth is that I'm working too much to enjoy the view," Jack replied, "but yeah, it is pretty special I guess, when you really think about it. I wouldn't start waxing lyrical about working in an office though. There's nothing glamorous about it. It looks better on the outside than it does on the inside, of that I have no doubt."

I smiled, but I disagreed with him. I couldn't think of anything better than working in one of those offices, of going into work every day with pride, knowing that you were doing something important and making a difference in the world. I always envied people who got to wear smart clothes to work. I always imagined they were treated with great respect. There used to be people who came by the orphanage who screamed success. It wasn't just in the clothes they wore, but also in the way they carried themselves. Jack had the same quality. I could tell, even though I hadn't seen his face yet.

I dragged my hands up around his spine and then spread my fingers out, pushing along the contours of his back. His skin was tone. I took note of the dusting of moles across his otherwise pale skin. His shoulders were broad, his neck sturdy. I moved his head from side to side as I worked my fingers along the nape of his neck and down to his shoulders, easing the tension away. A long, guttural groan escaped his lips. Sometimes Mark was right to worry, I thought. Sometimes this job was truly intimate.

"What made you decide to be a masseuse?" Jack asked. "It's an unusual career. Was it something you fell into?"

"Well... I grew up around a lot of kids and they tended to injure themselves a lot so I ended up taking care of them. I saw this job posting and Ally had me show her what I could do and that was that."

"Sounds simple enough. It must be relaxing to work in a place like this. It's so soothing."

"It is," I smiled, and I was genuine in my answer. This place was like a haven and even though I had the responsibility to make other people relax, it was calming to be in a room with gentle music playing and with a flowery scent rising in the air. Even though I wasn't being massaged I still felt that this room was an escape from whatever was stressing me out in my own life.

Mark.

"I'm just going to move to your head now," I said. He nodded. I ran my fingers through his thick hair, rubbing his scalp. He shuddered a little and I smiled with amusement. Most people didn't realize how much tension was carried in their head and they were amazed at the relief they felt from just a simple massage. I moved my hands to his temples and pressed my fingers against them. He lifted his head a little to allow me a better reach, but as I did so my sleeve rose and he saw the mark on my wrist.

"Is that a tattoo?" he asked.

I immediately pulled my hand away and my heart thumped in my chest. I cradled my arm and blinked away my surprise. The light was dim and he clearly hadn't seen it properly. My secret was still safe. God. I couldn't let the truth come out. Mark would be so upset if I failed him.

"Uh, yeah," I said quickly. "But it's pretty fresh so it's still sore. I'm sorry, I meant to keep it covered up."

"You don't have to apologize. I've always liked the idea of getting a tattoo, but I've never been able to think of one that fits. They're so final I suppose, and I've never seen one that I would be truly happy with. There was one idea I had when I was younger, which was to get a memento of all the places I traveled to in my life, so that when I came to my later years I could look back and my whole body would be like a map or a scrap book of where I had traveled. I always thought that would be a nice thing."

"What stopped you?" I asked, glad that the conversation had moved on swiftly.

"Oh, well I didn't travel as much as I thought I would. I mean, I have been to different countries, but I've mostly been stuck in board meetings and conferences. I haven't really experienced different places, you know, getting to the root of the local culture. I keep telling myself I have more time, but then another year passes and the dreams are delayed once again." He caught himself and laughed. "I'm sorry. I don't mean to get so melancholy. This is supposed to be a relaxing place, not a depressing one," he said.

"It's whatever you want it to be," I said diplomatically as I moved down to his legs, rubbing the balls of his feet before moving up to his calf muscles. Like the rest of his body he was strong, and although he spoke as though work was the most dominating force in his life I could tell that he put a lot into the upkeep of his body as well. I could tell a lot from a man about the way he treated his body, even the way he smelled. Sometimes I had to gag with men whose sweat was as greasy as the food they ate, but Jack smelled clean and fresh.

"That's a lovely sentiment. Have you had the chance to travel much?" Jack asked.

"I haven't. I think I'd like to because I never got the chance when I was younger, but my boyfriend doesn't like traveling too much. We've driven across the state a few times, but other countries? I'm afraid that he's too much of a patriot for that. According to him there's no point going anywhere else because America has everything we could ever want."

"Well, I suppose he has a point in a way," Jack said. "Does he not mind you working in a place like this?"

I swallowed a lump in my throat and felt myself getting flustered. I rarely talked about personal things with my clients, and they rarely asked. The most that happened was sometimes a guy would make some flirty comment and I politely reminded them that I was taken, but there was something different about Jack, something that I couldn't quite put my finger on. This scared me.

"It's just a job," I said. "I guess it's natural for anyone to have their reservations about it, it's only human, but he's okay. I mean, we have to do what we have to do to get by in this world, don't we?"

"That we do, and speaking of that I suppose it's time for the final part," he said, turning around. My oiled hands slipped off his flesh and he rolled over and arched his leg up. I caught a glimpse of the bulge underneath the towel. How thankful I was for that towel, shielding me from the most intimate part of him. My gaze helplessly moved up his body. I followed the narrow line of dark hair the burst into a masculine shadow across his broad chest and rippling muscles. Light stubble dusted his square jaw. His lips were full, his smile lazy, and his eyes filled with intent. He was mature, and yet at the same time there was something boyish about him as well. My entire body went rigid as I drew myself back, afraid of these feelings inside me, afraid of the forbidden things that might happen in this room, hidden from the world.

"I- I'm sorry if you got the... the wrong impression but we... we don't do that here," I said, the words tumbling out of me in an uncertain rhythm. I averted my gaze, hoping and praying that he would keep the towel pressed against his flesh. A knot tightened in my stomach. An instinctive, primal part of me wanted him to tear it away, but I was better than that. I was more than that. I was Mark's.

"Oh my goodness I'm so sorry," Jack said, as though it was the simplest of all misunderstandings. "I thought it might have been, well, no matter. I suppose not every story gets its happy ending," he said with a grin. I smiled nervously, still keeping my distance, afraid to touch him again. He swung his legs down and held the towel around his waist as he hopped off the table. "I'm sorry if I made you uncomfortable," he said.

"It's okay. It's not the first time this has happened," I replied. "I'll just go and get your bill ready if you'd like to get dressed." I blew out the candles and turned off the music. Instead of melodic music the room was now filled with the rustle of Jack getting dressed, my frantic footsteps, and the rising, awkward tension that came about as the result of his abrupt request. My heart thundered, not only because I had been taken by surprise, but also because part of me was curious about what hid underneath the towel. I wondered if it was as glorious as the rest of him, and then I instantly chastised myself for thinking such things. It was wrong. I shouldn't think about anyone else like that, not while I was with Mark. And yet Jack was so unlike anyone else I had ever met. He had a way of cutting through my defenses, but at least it was almost over. Soon enough he would walk out of this salon and out of my life and I'd never have to worry about him again.

Chapter Three

"Well, he's certainly not like the usual clientele we get," Ally said after Jack walked out of the salon, whistling nonchalantly as though nothing awkward had happened between us. I watched him disappear from view, and breathed a sigh of relief that it was all behind me. "I should have taken him for myself," Ally flashed a teasing smile. I returned one of my own as I washed the lotion off my hands.

"It wasn't all that good. He asked me for a happy ending," I said.

"No, really?" Ally gasped.

"Yeah, just rolled right around and asked me if it was time for the final part," I said. Ally giggled and clapped her hands together. She walked over to the till and pulled out a few notes, placing them in a jar. We put some money in this jar whenever anyone asked for a happy ending, and used the funds to pay for a Christmas outing at the end of every year. We always had a good time.

"I'm tempted to put up a sign in the window to stop this from happening again, but then our Christmases would be a lot less fun," Ally said.

I nodded along and looked at the jar, which was close to being half full. Sadly it was quite a common request, mostly from men. Sometimes they just needed a quick release of stress, while other times they were looking for something a little deeper; a touch of intimacy perhaps. Either they had lost that spark with their wives or their beds were barren and they tried to reclaim it here, in this house of noble repute. I wondered which choice was the case for Jack. I was convinced it was the former because I couldn't imagine his bed being barren, but I shook the thought from my mind because it wouldn't do me any good to think about that. The only uncommon thing about his request was my reaction to it. Never before had I actually been tempted to fulfill such a wish. Even just thinking about it made me feel guilt, as though I had actually cheated on Mark.

"Well, I'm glad he wasn't too insistent, and I'm glad it's not a choice you offer. I think Mark's head would explode if he thought I was doing something like that."

"Is he still giving you a hard time about working here?" Ally asked, her tone immediately turning sympathetic. I had confided in her, and Cindy, about some of the problems I experienced with Mark, because it was good to be able to share these problems with people, but sometimes I think they overreacted or took things I said to the extreme. They were given a skewed view of Mark because I mostly spoke about him whenever I had something to complain about, so they were seeing him in the very worst light and I take full responsibility for that. But I hated the way she tilted her head to the side and wore that look of concern, as though I was trapped in this awful thing that I couldn't escape.

"I don't think he's ever going to be happy about it," I replied, and then added quickly, "but that's only normal. I think I would feel the same if he was around scantily clad women all day. He had something special planned for today so he was annoyed that I had swapped shifts with Cindy."

"He didn't... do anything, did he?" Ally asked. I knew the meaning of her words.

"No," I lied, shaking my head even as my hand passed over my injured forearm.

"Well, that's something at least. Sandi, I don't mean to butt my nose in where it doesn't belong, but you know that you don't have to be with someone if you're unhappy with them, right? There's nothing that says we have to hold onto something that's not working."

"Mark and I are happy," I said defiantly, the words harsher than I intended them to be. "We just have our rough patches, like any other couple."

"Okay," Ally said warily, "I just don't want one of these rough patches to turn into something that you can't come back from. In some ways life can seem long, but it's very, very short and we only have a limited amount of time to make the right decisions. I care about you Sandi and I want to know that you're happy and safe."

"I am," I replied, forcing a smile. "Believe me, I know that Mark isn't the perfect guy, but if I wait around for perfection then I'm going to be waiting a long time. I'm not perfect either."

I knew that my words were going to fall on deaf ears. Ally just wasn't going to believe that I could be happy with Mark, but different people had different measures of happiness. Sure, I could have flung myself at Jack and likely made a fool of myself, but I learned a long time ago that the most consistent thing men do is leave. Mark was a lot of things, but at least I knew he was going to stick around. Painful memories started to come to the fore, memories that I had tried so hard to bury. I wish that I could wrench them out of my soul, but they always came back, haunting me like a lingering spirit, waiting to taunt and torment me and remind me that I'm just a worthless nobody.

*

I was fifteen, old enough to know better, but young enough not to care. By this point I had given up on ever being adopted. There was an understanding around everyone in the foster world that once you reached a certain age that was it. Sure, a few rare people found kind hearted souls who were willing to take a young adult into their homes, but mostly people wanted the cute button nosed little girls or the precocious cheeky boys, not some teenager with a chip on her shoulder and an attitude that only meant trouble. I was in purgatory, waiting to turn eighteen, when I would be released to the world and forced to make my own way to the future.

"How do you feel about it?" Patrick asked. He was long and lean. His voice was smooth; it reached down to my soul. His eyes were like the sea, and inspired plenty of bad poetry on my part. We'd grown up together, watched other kids get chosen over us, and with each rejection our bond got stronger. Back then I was so sure that we were going to be together forever. I didn't know what the future held, but I knew that we were going to meet it head on, because we were a team. We were the ones everyone looked to for guidance. All the kids knew that we were the king and queen of the place, and the adults treated us with respect because we could keep the troublesome ones in line. My young, tender heart yearned for him. His was the most beautiful soul, and it felt as though he was all the missing parts of me.

"I don't know. I guess it'll be nice to get out of here. I have no idea what I'm going to do though."

"It doesn't matter what we do, only that we do it together," he said. He always had a way of making the impossible real. When we spoke of our dreams they weren't simply ethereal things, they were tangible, there hanging from the branch and all we had to do was reach up and pluck them. In Patrick's mind it was all just a matter of time until we had everything we deserved, and damn I had been waiting a long time.

I smiled shyly, my hair falling across my face like a veil. We were sitting in our special place, a bench under a shaded tree that was as old as time, its roots buried deep in the ground. Here we could escape into a world of our own making, a cocoon of... well, of love. Neither of us had said it yet. Hell, we were still so awkward that the most we amounted to was smiling shyly at each other, and yet we both knew we felt it. That was the important part. It was warm and electric and I just knew that when I was with him anything was possible. It felt like a fire burned inside me. Every time I look at him I lit up, and when he wasn't around the world was a little dimmer.

"You seem so sure of it," I said gently, worried that the moment would crack under the strain of my hopes and dreams.

"I am," he replied, his words deep and prophetic, as though he was peering beyond the veil of the world to gaze at the future. "I see us together, making our way in the world, putting all this behind us. I want to see it all with you Sandi. I want to travel the world and leave no stone unturned. I don't care how we make money, I don't want to build a fortune, I want to build a life. I want to build memories."

"I want that too," I said, but I never got to finish my sentence. The words have been lost to time as my breath was suffocated with the most beautiful kiss there had ever been. My first kiss. Idyllic and glorious, intoxicating and addictive, my toes curled and all my insides turned to jelly. The world turned upside down and a part of me knew that I would never see it in the same way again. Even now I can feel his hand sliding across my cheek, the hunger in his lips, the warmth of his breath rippling over me like a wave. In that moment I would have given him absolutely anything. I was ready to give him my future, my life. It was all his to take.

Our hands clasped together as we took the first tentative steps into love, shedding our innocence. Our pasts were turbulent and stormy, but our future was paved with gold and there seemed no way for us to fail.

But paradise was an illusion. Dreams never lasted too long. A miracle happened and Patrick had been chosen to be fostered by a family who lived on the other side of the city. I could tell that he was happy and I was happy for him, but at the same time I felt him slipping away and all I wanted was for him to stay. This wasn't right. We were supposed to stay together. We had been together all this time and now... now he was just going to leave? It didn't seem fair. I couldn't stop the tears from falling down. He held me all night, rocking me in his arms, promising me that nothing was going to change that much. We were still going to see each other. He'd visit me, and when I had enough money I could get the bus through the city to see him, or we could meet in the middle.

At the time I believed him, but I quickly learned that promises were easily given and hardly kept. At first he was eager to call me and text me, but those quickly faded away as he was seduced by the opportunities of his new life. The pain in my heart was so great that I honestly thought

I was going to die. We had planned to do so much and then it all just came to a crashing end. I felt sick. I was no good to anyone. The other kids tried to help me, but nobody could say anything. The adults told me that it would get better in time and that there would be other chances to fall in love, but he was my first chance and my best chance and I didn't want to stop loving him.

But I had to.

I kept waiting for the day when he returned. Every time there was a new visitor I looked up, unable to stop hope from flickering to life inside me, and every time it was doused by cold reality. I watched other kids get taken away, rescued from this purgatory, but I remained. Time ticked by and I waited until it was my time to leave, but something broke inside me. Something pure and wonderful was tainted and stained, and I knew I wasn't going to be good for anyone. My birth parents hadn't wanted me. No foster family wanted me. Even Patrick didn't want me.

Had it all been lies?

Everything he said... the kiss... it had all been an illusion. It had all just been something to pass the time and it was clear that I hadn't meant as much to him as he had meant to me. When I looked into his eyes and thought I saw something special I realized that I had just been seeing the reflection of my own feelings. He hadn't meant a word of it.

Eventually it came time for me to leave. I was unleashed into the world and I had always assumed that I would be taking these steps with Patrick by my side, but he was just a ghost of a memory now. My heart was a cold stone as I took my first steps into the world. I made my way into the city, wondering if Patrick was still around, wondering if there was a part of him that remembered me.

Another truth I learned is that fate can be cruel. One day I was minding my own business when suddenly I saw him. He wore different clothes and his hair was shorter. He looked more like he fit into this world, but it was him all the same. It felt like a lightning bolt lanced through me. The crowd melted away as I walked up to him. For so long I had thought about what I had wanted to say to him, how I wanted to tell him how much his betrayal had stung and how many nights had been sleepless because of him. I wanted to unleash all my fury, and yet at the same time I just wanted to fling my arms around him and tell him what sweet torture it had been to be apart from him. I started to think that perhaps there had been another explanation. Maybe his foster parents had been cruel and forced him to cut ties with his past. Maybe we were still meant to be together, still meant to seize our future together against all the odds. I could feel all the possibilities converge, rushing in a torrent towards me.

I called out his name. He turned to face me. A flicker of recognition appeared in his eyes and love swelled in my heart. A smile spread across my face. Oh, Patrick, how wrong I had been to doubt you. How foolish I had been to give up on our love. I was giddy. The world was spinning.

Then suddenly it came to an abrupt stop.

"Who is this?" a voice asked with derision. Somehow I had missed her, but she had been there all the time. Beautiful and petite, she had deep red hair where mine was light brown. Her curves were voluptuous while I was taller and slender. Her clothes were clean and fit perfectly while mine were the same ragged ones I had always worn. Her nails were manicured, her lips shone like rubies, and she appeared to be a part of this world. As did he. I was still on the outside but he had changed. He had been assimilated and now belonged, with his crisp shirt and beige trousers. She hung on his arm, glaring at me, protecting what she had lay claim to.

Patrick's eyes glazed over and I knew that was the last I had ever seen of the boy I had known and loved.

"I don't know," he said. Then, he looked me directly in the eye and he shattered whatever tiny fragments were left of my heart. "I'm sorry, I think there's been a mistake. I don't know who you are."

He walked away without giving me a chance to respond, taking my future with him.

Chapter Four

"What are you thinking about?" Mark asked as we relaxed on the couch.

"Just thinking of the past, you know, my life before you," I sighed, trying to quell the anguish that rose within me.

Mark smirked. "You had no life before me," he said. Part of that was true I suppose. I certainly didn't have fond memories of the past, and I hadn't told him about Patrick. Not everything anyway. He would only get angry that I had loved somebody before him, as though I was supposed to know that eventually we would meet and hold on until then.

"What do you love most about me Mark," I asked.

Mark smirked and barely took his eyes off the TV. "Everything," he said. "Especially this." He grabbed the curve of my ass and I smiled. He had never been shy in taking what he wanted.

"The thing I love about you is that I know you're going to stick around." I nestled my head into his chest, feeling comfort in the security of his body. "I know that you're never going to leave me."

"Hell no babe. I'm with you until the end of line, unless you do anything to disappoint me," he added the words of warning. I ignored them, as I always did, trying to find the romance hidden amongst his words.

"I mean it Mark. I really appreciate that I can depend on you. I've had so few things to depend on in life. I'm glad I have you. I want us to build a future together," I said.

"We will honey, all in good time. We just have to wait for the good times to come to us," he said.

I thought about my brief chat with Jack earlier as well. "I know, but I was thinking that we could do something to take matters into our own hands as well. I thought maybe we could take a trip somewhere exotic. You know, I mean, we've managed to save a little bit and it would be good to get out of the city. This place can get so suffocating all the time. I'm tired of seeing the same old places and the same people. I want to experience something new. Before we know it time has slipped away from us and we're not going to be able to do all these things we want to do," I said, my words gentle and imploring because Mark always hated it when I whined or demanded anything of him, but I hoped that he would at least be able to feel the genuine yearning in my voice.

He sighed. "Babe, you know we've talked about this before. I just don't want to leave the country. America has everything we could ever want, but I get what you're saying. Why don't you have a look at places we can stay along the coast or something? A trip would be nice, but you know life is all about compromises and I just don't want to leave the country. People don't like Americans you know. They're jealous of us and they think we're dumb. I don't want to go somewhere and they treat me like some kind of fool. It's better that we stay here, where we know people are going to treat us with respect."

"Okay," I sighed, knowing there was no use in arguing with him because he had made his mind up about it.

"But look, maybe when you're older and our kids are old enough you could take them for a trip over there," he said.

My ears pricked up. It was rare to hear about him speak of children, but when he did it filled me with mixed feelings. The thought of having a child of my own, to be able to give someone the love and devotion that I had been deprived of was overwhelming and yet the way Mark treated me... could I condemn someone else to that fate? It seemed like an impossible choice sometimes.

"You've been thinking about kids?" I asked.

"Sure have," Mark said. "Danny was talking about spending time at the weekends with his daughter and he's taken to fatherhood really well. He said it was the most magical thing that has ever happened to him and it's really changed his life. I guess now it seems like the done thing. I mean, it's what people do, isn't it? Plus Mom has been hounding me to have a grandchild and really, we'd better get started soon, otherwise, it's going to be more difficult, what with your biological clock and all. I want to do some research though because I want to figure out how we can increase our chances of getting a son. I mean, a girl would be fine and all, but I really want a Mark Jr., someone who can be exactly like me, but better too. I want them to drive forward and make something of themselves, like a ball player or something, then we can live out an easy retirement basking in their glory."

"What if they don't want to do that?"

Mark laughed and shook his head. "Why would anyone not want to be a ball player," he asked, laughing, and then turned to kiss me, the kind of kiss that was hard and fast and didn't show me any kind of tenderness at all. "In fact why don't we start now?" he whispered, his hands wrapping around me like claws.

*

I wasn't about to stop taking the pill just yet. I sat in bed, drawing my knees into my chest. Mark lay asleep, falling into slumber so easily. Shadows danced upon his chest. The blanket was pulled halfway down and his arms splayed out to the side. His head lolled and his mouth hung open, so ungraceful, so vulnerable. Sometimes when he was like this I imagined what it would be like to twist his wrist until he screamed. Some nights I was tempted more than anything, and I think I would have if I didn't know that the pain would be returned to me even more intensely. When he slept it seemed impossible to be afraid of him, but afraid I was.

I ran my hands through my hair, tugging at my scalp. My body trembled and I swallowed a lump in my throat that would never disappear. I couldn't stop thinking about what he had said earlier. Suddenly I could see the next few years pouring out in front of me. If I didn't get pregnant he'd say there was something wrong with me, something defective. If I gave birth to a girl he'd say that I did something wrong. Either way the child would be placed in his path, ready to be a victim. Part of me wanted to believe that he would change, that it would be different with a child, but I knew men like him wouldn't change. But if I was so afraid of making a child a victim of him, then why was I so eager to make excuses for him and stick with him?

I couldn't leave him. I knew that for sure. He was all I had and there was no way I was going to go back to being on my own again. I couldn't take it. I couldn't handle it. I needed to have someone to rely on and for all his faults Mark helped make sure that all the bills were paid and that there was a roof over my head. I thought about the yellow toothed homeless woman I had seen earlier. It was so easy to fall into something like that. I wasn't like Patrick. I couldn't just adjust to life in the city as though it was the easiest thing going. I buried my head in my hands and suddenly my palms were wet with sobs. I kept quiet, not wanting to wake Mark or bother him with my emotions. Why was my life like this? What had I done to deserve being treated like this?

A thought struck a chord in my heart, as clear as a bell. Would a child one day ask the same questions? It seemed irresponsible to bring a child into a world that was so filled with chaos. What had been going through my parents' mind when they had given me up? I bet they thought they were saving me when they gave me up for adoption. I bet they assumed that someone else was going to come along and take on the burden of me, but nobody ever had. I was just a forgotten girl. How was I going to be a mother when something inside me was broken?

Chapter Five

I left for work early the next morning, not wanting to wake Mark. I left him a note on the counter along with some breakfast, knowing that he would appreciate a gesture like this. I told him that the night had been wonderful, even though I couldn't stop thinking about the twisting doubts in my mind. I marched towards work, hoping that I would be able to lose myself in the rhythm of massage and push my mind away. Cindy and I had the run of the place today as Ally took a well deserved day off. Cindy greeted me with a smile.

"Thanks for covering for me yesterday, I hope Mark wasn't too upset," she said.

"Oh, it was okay. You know how Mark gets. He doesn't like plans being changed at the last minute, but we worked it out and things were fine. How was your Mom's birthday?"

"She loved it! Yeah, she had a great time," Cindy's face lit up with delight, and I was glad I had played a small part in it. "I hated to take the day off, but Mom has always loved her birthday and since Dad died, well, it's been left up to me to make it special. Not that I mind though, it's nice to do these things for her. How was work, I hope you didn't have any difficult clients?"

"No..." my mind drifted back towards Jack and all the complicated attraction I felt. "There was just one that stood out, this guy who thought we were a place who did happy endings," I laughed.

"Oh God, well, I'm glad I wasn't here for that. What was he like, old and flabby?"

"No, actually he was pretty young. Probably mid-thirties I'd say. He works in the city, said he was just down here to release some stress. He was quite nice actually, and he treated the happy ending as a joke. I don't think he'll be back again though," I admitted.

"Well, maybe so. You never know Sandi, you still might meet the man of your dreams here," she said.

I frowned and laughed in disbelief. "What are you talking about? I have Mark."

"Yeah, but come on, Mark is Mark. He's not going to be around forever. He's like the stop gap boyfriend you have in your twenties so you don't have to spend the best years of your life alone, but then someone else comes along," she said as though it was obvious. She saw the look of confusion on my face and stared at me as though I was stupid for not knowing this beforehand.

"Mark isn't just a stopgap," I protested.

Cindy placed her hands on her hips. "Then what is he?" she asked forcefully.

"I..." I began, searching for the words that would make everything clear, but there was something about me that couldn't answer the question as easily as I should have been able to. "We were just talking about the future and having kids." I said, as though that was the only answer that was required.

"Kids, really?" Cindy asked. Her hands dropped to her side and she had that same look that Ally had worn, that look of misplaced concern, worried that things were worse than they seemed.

"You don't have to say it like that," I said, folding my arms across my body in a defensive posture. "We've been going out for a few years now and it's only natural that we should think about the future. I know that you and Ally don't like him, and believe me I know that he's acted like a jerk in the past, but the one thing he's done that nobody else has is stand by me, and that counts for something. So yes, we've been talking about having kids and there's nothing wrong with that." The words burst from me in a rat a tat rhythm.

"Because he knows he's not ever going to do better than you," Cindy muttered under her breath, but held up her hands in surrender when she saw the glare on my face. "Okay, okay, I'm sorry," she said. "I didn't mean to disparage your relationship. I just think... it doesn't matter. So, what did you talk about? Are you going to try for one?"

And just like that we slipped into our natural friendly rhythm. Of course, I felt a little like a fraud for having to back away and not reveal the truth that I was having my doubts. I suppose I could have lied, but I felt isolated enough without keeping my troubles to myself.

"I don't know," I admitted. "I was thinking about it and I do like the idea of having a kid, but it's such a big responsibility and the way Mark is... I just feel like he has a lot of maturing to do before he's ready for a kid. Like, it's one thing getting angry at me when I do something he doesn't like, but he can't be that way with a kid. It's not fair."

"No, it's not, although you know it's not fair to you either, right?" Cindy asked. I glared at her again and decided to ignore the question.

"I guess I'm just afraid that everything is changing and I don't know what I'm supposed to be doing. I wish I had everything figured out. I used to think that when I was older I'd get to a point where everything made sense, but if such a point exists I am still waiting to reach it."

"I don't think it ever happens. We just muddle through as best we can," Cindy said. At this point the door opened and one of Cindy's regulars came in. "Look, I want to talk about this more. I get the feeling you have a lot to get off your chest. Why don't you come out with me tomorrow night? We can get a few drinks and have a dance, really let off some steam. It'll be fun. Blake is DJ'ing at this fancy club. I'm sure he won't mind getting you in either. We haven't been on a girl's night out in forever."

My heart leapt at the thought, but the flame of excitement was quickly extinguished with the knowledge of what Mark would say.

"I'd love to, but I just don't think it's a good idea right now..." I trailed off, averting my gaze.

"Because of Mark?" Cindy asked sharply. She greeted her client with a smile and told him to wait in the massage parlor. She hissed at me before she left. "You can't let him stop you from having fun Sandi. Come on, this is your life. You have every right to live it."

With that sentiment left like the microphone on a rap battle stage she walked away to tend to her client. For the rest of the day I was left thinking on her words and the prospect of letting my hair down for a night. The clients came and went. I lost myself in a sea of strange flesh, oddly intimate for a period of time, and then they would clothe themselves and return to their normal lives while I would wash the lotion and the sweat off my palms. How many men had I touched like this over the years? Was Mark right to be worried? Was this one step away from being a whore? It was less intimate than sex, but more intimate than a medical examination and although I didn't usually feel stirrings of arousal within my heart for my clients, there were times when it happened, like with Jack. I could still feel the contours of his muscles underneath my fingers, running like the valleys of a landscape, so broad and vast I could throw myself into it and be lost in another world. Was Cindy right? Were there better options for me out there? I had never been able to conceive of them before because any time I hoped, it had always ended in disappointment, but she was right in one thing. I was going to have to change if I wanted to be happy. I couldn't always let Mark walk over me, and if he was going to be the father of my child he was going to have to prove it. Before I left I told her to tell Blake to get me on the guest list because I wanted in. We were going to have a girl's night out, and it was going to be amazing.

Chapter Six

"You can't go! I forbid it!" Mark yelled. I had just told him that I was going out with Cindy and he had reacted with his usual exuberance. The arms flailed out. The nostrils flared. The eyes were filled with rage and the air around him simmered as though some monster had just been unleashed.

"You forbid it? Mark, you can't stop me from spending time with my friends," I shot back, my pride not allowing me to acquiesce to his demands, even though I knew that pain was likely to follow.

"I can if I think it's going to be safer for you, and Cindy isn't a friend, she's just someone you work with. It's bad enough that you had to swap shifts with her to ruin our day together, but now you're going to ruin our whole weekend as well? Do you even want to take a trip or do you just want to party? Why would you even want to do this?" he asked.

"Cindy invited me for a night out and I thought it would be fun to do something different. I don't make this kind of fuss when you go out with your buddies."

"Yeah, because my buddies and I don't dress in barely anything and we don't go out to dance where people can ogle at us and leer at us. We have some beers and a laugh and that's it. It's simple and it's clean and I don't have any guys drooling over me."

"You don't have to worry about that. You can trust me."

"Oh, I trust you just fine, it's them I don't trust," he pointed a thick finger in the general direction of outside, at all these men who were supposedly interested in me. Sometimes it was sweet, how protective he was and how he thought that every man was going to be after me. The reality was far different, but why couldn't he see that?

"Nothing is going to happen. We're going to have a little dance and a few drinks and that's it. I'll probably be home before you usually get home."

"Don't try and turn this around on me," Mark said, shaking his head and pacing around like a caged bull. "Where even are you going?"

"It's a party that Blake is playing. You remember him, he's Cindy's DJ friend?"

"Oh yeah, great, some fancy party and you're just going to be there on the dance floor and everyone is going to think they can take their turn." He thought for a moment. "How about I come with you," he said.

"Mark, come on," I threw up my hands. "The whole point is that it's supposed to be a girl's night out."

"Fine, fine, then I'll choose what you wear."

"Whatever, fine, if it'll make you feel more comfortable," I said. It was another concession that I knew I shouldn't have to make. I could almost hear Ally and Cindy's sighs, a pitying chorus in the back of my mind, but I ignored it as I went into the bedroom and flung open my closet. Mark started to rummage through my clothes and pulled out a few outfits he thought were suitable, but all of them were frumpy, unflattering, and totally not what anyone would wear to a club.

"Come on Mark, be realistic," I said. "You can't expect me to wear these things."

"And what are you thinking of wearing?" he asked. I rose from the bed and pushed past him, reaching in to pull out some yellow hot pants and a cream colored top that clasped around my neck, leaving my shoulders and the sides of my body exposed. It was one of my favorite tops and had been something I bought for myself after I'd saved some money. Buying things with money I earned was one of the few joys I had. It felt good to be able to exert control over something like that.

"How about this?" I asked.

Mark took it and frowned, then laughed as if I had presented him with a joke. "This? This? Are you kidding me Sandi? Do you know what men are going to think when they see you in this? I know how men think. You might not know, but they're going to think you're in play and they're not going to stop. The next thing you know they're going to be all up in you and offering to buy you drinks and touching everywhere," he winced and threw the outfit down, gagging on the revulsion of it all. "No, I can't take it. I can't handle it. It's bad enough that you have to spend your days touching other men, but at least you're getting paid for it. I'm not going to have you go to this club and be treated like a piece of meat. Come on Sandi, I'm only doing this for your own good. Why would you want to wear something like this?"

"Because I want to look good!"

"For who? For them?" he glared, furious at the idea I would want to appeal to the opposite sex. I rolled my eyes.

"Not for them. For me," I sagged on the bed, fretful sobs dripping out of me. I pushed back a whole handful of hair and sighed, gnawing on my lower lip. "This is what you don't understand. None of those men matter. I'm not going to let any of them dance with me because I don't want them to dance with me. Why can't you trust me in this Mark? All I want is to go out for one night and enjoy myself with my friend because I don't have many of them. I rarely have. I'm not like you. I don't have a group from high school I'm going to be friends with for the rest of my life. Nights like this are rare for me and I just want to be able to go out knowing that you don't have a problem with it. Please..." I begged, searching his eyes for sympathy. For a moment I thought I was going to get it, but just like with Patrick when I saw him in the city the thing that flickered in his eyes was gone, and left was a man I didn't understand. Mark flung down the outfit as though he was casting it to hell.

"If you want to go then go, but I'm never going to approve of you going to a place like that. Men are men. They're beasts. They're not going to care that you're with someone else. They're not even going to ask the question, and once you've had a few drinks you'll be a target for any of them. Just the thought of you there... it drives me crazy!" he yelled as he stormed out of the room and thumped through the house. I looked at all the clothes he had pulled out of the closet and sighed, wondering if Cindy and Ally were right. Did I have to put up with this? It was as though everything I wanted to do had to be some kind of a fight. Nothing was ever easy, and I just didn't have the energy to battle him constantly. But what about in the future? What about when it came to the matter of our child? No... I couldn't just let him run roughshod over me. I had to make a stand. This may not have been the noblest or most honorable thing to take a stand on, but I was determined to go out with Cindy.

I collected my emotions and then walked through the house, finding him looking out of the window, staring at nothing in particular. It wasn't as though we had a pleasant view.

"Mark, you can't just run away every time we have an argument. Come on, you know I'd never let anything like that happen."

"Leave me Sandi. I'm not going to say it again. I'm pissed off right now and I'm just about able to keep my emotions in check but if you goddamned say one more word-"

"Mark," I said gently, reaching out towards him to try and get him to face me. I wanted to tell him that he didn't have to be this way, that he didn't have to react with such anger to everything I wanted to do, but he lashed out and struck me across the face. I was flung to the floor, sinking under the shock and the impact of his blow. Pain bloomed over my cheek, rippling as though a stone skimmed a clear lake. My mouth hung open and tears stung my eyes.

"You bastard," I said, "you can't do this Mark. You can't keep lashing out at me when you can't control your own emotions," I said, pushing myself away from him.

"I warned you. I fucking warned you," he pointed at me, towering over me like a giant. The fear was familiar now, like a companion guiding me through this horror. "I already told you that you could go. If you want to disrespect me and all that we've built together then fine. If you want to dress up like a whore that's fine too, but don't come crying to me when some guy puts his hands on you and you're not able to resist him. And just so we're straight, I'm not going to put up with damaged goods," he spat. There were times when I could look past his rigid demeanor to find the kindness within, but then there were times like these when he just looked ugly, when there was no drop of goodness in him at all.

"You can't do this," I gasped, still shaking my head. "God Mark... you can't talk about kids one day and then do this to me. You have to stop. I won't let you do this to my kid."

Mark's face twisted in horror. He leaned forward, peering at me, looking as though the moon was rushing down from the sky. "You think I'd do this to a kid? Fuck Sandi, what kind of man do you think I am? I ain't no kid beater. I ain't no wife beater either you just... GOD you just make so damned mad sometimes. I don't know why you can't just listen to me and do the things I tell you to do. I only want what's best for you. Why can't you see that?"

"Because sometimes I want to be allowed to make mistakes and have some freedom. I'm your girlfriend Mark, not your prisoner. This is just one night out," I said, rubbing my cheek in the hope that the pain would fade, but I knew it would last a while longer. "Nothing is going to happen and this didn't even have to be an argument if you didn't react like this. You have to control your temper. If we have a kid and they don't do something you approve of what are you going to do then?"

"They'd never do anything like that because I'll teach them to respect me," he spat. I knew what kind of respect he meant and it made me sick. I hung my head and groaned.

"That's not how life works Mark. You can't just expect things of people. They're going to make mistakes and when they do you have to treat them with compassion and kindness, otherwise they'll just stop coming to you. I don't want our kids to be afraid of you."

"Fear isn't a bad thing. It'll keep them in line," he said, without any irony at all.

At that point I didn't know what to do. He clearly had a way of living in his mind and nothing else was suitable, but it seemed wrong to me. I couldn't just let this be the end of it. I couldn't allow a child to be condemned to this.

"I'm still going out with Cindy," I said.

"Good. I hope that it doesn't lead to anything bad happening to you."

I knew he meant it as a warning, but I couldn't help but feel as though it was a threat as well. I stayed on my knees, rocking back and forth, caught between my fear of being alone and my anxiety of the future. I always just assumed that one day Mark would realize that what he's doing is wrong, but he's so convinced that this is the way forward I can't do anything to stop him. He's just... he's stubborn and frightful and there doesn't seem to be any way I can change his mind, but then what does that mean for me? How am I supposed to just leave him?

Eventually I dragged myself off the floor and went to the kitchen to put some ice on my cheek. I never wanted my life to turn out like this, but perhaps it was all I deserved. Maybe it was better to live in fear of someone, than of them leaving. Cindy and Ally might not approve of the way Mark treats me, but nothing he's done has ever hurt me as much as what Patrick did. The way he walked away, the way he pretended he didn't know me, cut me deep, and I was never going to let that happen again. That's what Ally and Cindy didn't understand. If I allowed myself to believe that I could truly love someone I would be opening myself up to a world of hurt that I could never come back from. Deep down I knew that I was with Mark for convenience as much as anything else. Love only played a small part in our relationship, but people stayed together for less. And perhaps Mark was right; maybe he would be different with a kid, maybe I could take the blows for them.

I still wasn't sure if I could take that chance, but it gave me pause for thought.

I just wanted to get out there with Cindy and let my hair down. For one night I wanted to pretend like I had my life in order, like I knew what I was doing. I thought about Jack and how confident he had seemed, even when he had been lying there draped in nothing but a towel. There was something knotted deep within him that spoke to his swagger and his command of the world. He was probably about ten years older than me and he seemed the type of man who had his life all figured out. It must have been so easy to be him. I bet he didn't have a worry in the world.

Chapter Seven

I rubbed my temples, just like that girl at the massage parlor did, but somehow it didn't have the same effect. Damn she had the magic touch. I'd felt better after seeing her than I had done in years. In less than an hour she had undone years of tension that had built up in my body, knotting me together, as though someone had poured concrete inside. The way she touched me had been more intimate than I was expecting, and even though it had been a couple of days since the massage I hadn't been able to stop thinking about it. Of course, given everything that was happening, the tension had all come back and her good work had been undone within minutes, but I appreciated the respite anyway. I closed my eyes and tried to ignore the thrum behind them, or the way it felt like my head was going to explode. I was still annoyed at myself for turning around and assuming that it was a massage with a happy ending. The way she touched me, so sensual and slow, I assumed it was. Guess I can't show my face around there any longer, which is a shame really as she was kind of cute. She had potential at least.

"Mr. Easter, your father is on line one," Shelley called through the intercom. The tension just increased. I groaned as I picked up the receiver, letting out a long exhalation of breath.

"Hey Dad," I said.

"Jack my boy, good, good," my father's gruff voice came through clearly on the phone. "I've just been looking through the papers and I've seen some very interesting movement in the stock market I think you should take a look at. Now, I know what you're going to say, so don't even worry about saying it; just take an old man's wisdom for what it's worth. I've forgotten more about this company than you will ever learn and I'm not going to be told that I'm old and useless."

"Nobody is saying that," I sighed. As usual, I was amazed at how Dad could conjure up an argument when he was the only one talking. It astounded me how anyone had managed to work with him when he was this irascible. But then again it had been a different time, when business had been conducted behind closed doors within a cabal of men who all shared the same outlook. Now there was a much more nuanced dynamic and there were more than a few people shaping the world, not that his father, would understand that.

"You're thinking it. I know that much for sure. I've heard what they're saying about me you know. They think old Garrett has lost it, but they don't understand. They don't have the instinct for business like I do. They're just jealous."

"I'm sure they are Dad, so go ahead, what are these stock options you've seen?" I rested the phone against my shoulder and yawned as he listed the ideas he had. It was easier to humor him than to try and fight. I had to stop him about halfway through.

"Dad, all the companies you've just mentioned have had their stocks plummet. They're not viable options at all," I said.

Dad muttered something under his breath. I couldn't quite catch what it was, but I knew it wasn't anything complimentary.

"That's precisely why they caught my attention. These are reputable names son, they're too big to fail and it's only a matter of time before their value surges back up. We need to strike now while the price is what it is. We have the opportunity and we must take it!"

"Dad, nothing is too big to fail. These companies are all involved in things that are becoming less important in the world. Look, I appreciate the call and I understand that you're just trying to help, but we have an entire department of people looking at the stock market so I don't think you're going to find something they miss. You should be resting and relaxing. This is your retirement. You've earned this Dad."

"Yeah, well, it's not the same without your Mom," Garrett grumbled. A moment of tension passed between us as Mom was mentioned. We rarely spoke about her because it was too painful and yet her ghost still haunted our memories.

"I know Dad, I know. I miss her too."

Grief turned to anger immediately. "And what are you doing about it?"

"What do you mean?"

"You know damned well what I mean Jack. Why aren't you out there looking for a wife? You can't spend the rest of your life alone. What about the legacy of a business? What about your own sanity?"

"Believe me Dad I would be happy to have a wife if the right woman came along, but I just haven't met her yet."

"Time is running out Jack, believe you me. You can't always think that one day it's just going to magically happen because the world doesn't work like that. I worked too much and Shelley put up with it all because I kept promising her that one day she would have me all to herself, but I took too long to retire and then she died before we could fully enjoy it. We don't have the luxury of time Jack. You need to get your ass in gear."

"I will Dad," I said.

We spoke for a little more time. He grumbled about the live in carer I had for him before I told him I had to get back to work. It was always the same though. I thought that being lectured about finding a wife would have disappeared when Mom died, but Dad had taken up that particular baton. I understood where they were coming from but I simply didn't have room in my life for that kind of thing. I'd tried relationships before, but none of them had been able to accept the rigorous schedule of my life. Sometimes I felt like they expected me to give up my business for them. Oh, of course, at first they were all impressed at how I managed the family business and had seen it grow throughout the years, but when it came to the reality of my life they were disappointed. There seemed to be a cognitive dissonance in them; they saw my wealth and my position in society, yet they seemed to think I could rest on my laurels and relax, as though it all appeared out of nowhere and now would manage itself. I had to manage it. I had to keep it running smoothly else it was liable to fall apart, but since I had so much to manage already how was I ever going to hold a relationship together?

Despite my best efforts I couldn't get that girl Sandi out of my mind. It was rare for someone to make such an impression on me. Through all the meetings of the day she kept drifting through my mind. At the thought of her my muscles unwound, as though she was plying my flesh with her talented fingers once again, draining the tension from me. Well, not all the tension. I laughed a little at my faux pas. I guess I wouldn't be showing my face there again.

My day was filled with meetings. They came one after the other, boring meetings filled with boring people who all had interchangeable faces. Sometimes I wondered if I had been cursed with this life, and all I wanted to do was walk out of there and do something exciting. But some things were bigger than a single life. I was but a steward ushering this company, making sure that it remained buoyant and one day I would hand off the reins to... to...

After the meetings my assistant reminded me that there was an upcoming event that required my attendance. I scowled as the last thing I wanted was to socialize with people at this vapid function. It was a distraction to my routine, yet necessary to attend for the sake of appearances. The nuances of social life were often draining and I think the world would be a better place if we were more honest with each other. I decided to go for a run and clear my mind. The effects of the massage had barely lasted a day before the tension began to build inside me once again. Such is my life I suppose; there's never a moment to relax.

I walked out of my last meeting with a dark cloud in my mind. In my office I changed into my exercise clothes and jogged away from the towering skyscraper towards the park along the harbor, where the dappled sunlight danced upon a glittering sea. I saw people playing with their children and wondered if that fate would ever befall me. I had always imagined that I would end up with a child one day because it seemed inevitable, as though it was an inexorable truth of the universe that everyone would procreate and a child would just appear out of thin air, but of course that wasn't true. Dad expected me to continue the family legacy. Hell, I expected myself to do the same. The last thing I wanted was for the company to fall into the hands of some interloper, or worse, one of my useless cousins. Dad was wrong though. I still had plenty of time to change things. Life is getting longer for everyone, and being in my thirties was still like being in my twenties.

I shook the thoughts from my mind, telling me to not let the old man get in my head. I knew who I was and I knew where I was going. Unlike most in this life I didn't have to worry about figuring out my life's path or purpose. There was no existential crisis plaguing me and I didn't have to run away from everything to 'find myself'. Such a thing was a waste of time, and only done by people who didn't know how to apply themselves properly to a project. Everything would fall into place, just as it had done so far. When it's time for me to find a wife I will find one, because I am the master of my own destiny and I shape the world to the way I see fit. I am not going to let Dad think that I do not get what I want, because I always do.

Chapter Eight

My heart fluttered as I got dressed. Mark glared and scowled at me, shaking his head and making his distaste clear. He had tried apologizing in his sweet beseeching tone. For a moment I actually believed he was sincere, before I insisted that I was going and all the sweetness evaporated from his face, his expression suddenly becoming bitter and acrid. He was trying to make me feel guilty and I told him that I wasn't going to have it. Why should I feel guilty for wanting to go out and have a good time with a friend? It frustrated me so much that every little thing had to be this drama. If he just said 'Sure Sandi, no problem, you go out and have a good time,' there would be no need for us to have these arguments and for this stress to rise within me. God I wish I could massage myself properly.

"So, you're going then," Mark said as I gathered my purse and waited for Cindy to arrive.

"Yes, Mark, I'm still going, and I don't want to hear you make some last ditch effort to try and get me to stay because it's not going to work"

"No, it's fine, I just think it's interesting how you're happy to spend a night out dancing instead of inside with the man you supposedly love."

"I do love you Mark," I said, although it was starting to sound like I was saying it out of habit rather than anything else. "There's nothing wrong with me wanting to spend one night out with Cindy. Believe me, I could do much worse."

"Is that a threat?" Mark glared at me.

"Forget I said anything. It's just a slip of the tongue," I sighed. "Look, just enjoy the night to yourself and I'll see you when I get back."

"Fine. I'll sit here thinking of a way you can make this up to me," he said.

I shook my head and left when the car horn beeped, glad to be out of that cauldron of emotion for one night. I opened the door and let the cool air bathe me. It swept away a lot of the tension that had risen within me. But surely I shouldn't have felt this relieved at leaving my own home? I worried that there was something deeply wrong, something that could not be fixed. As I walked towards the cab a knot of tension coiled around my heart and squeezed. The fear of being alone again flashed through me, but I managed to push it away as I joined Cindy.

She looked beautiful. She wore a sparkling black dress that looked as though stars had been stitched into the fabric. Her short black hair curved around her face, caressing her chin. She smiled and hugged me.

"I'm glad you could make it! This is going to be so much fun!" she said. "Mark didn't give you any trouble did he?"

"No, Mark was fine about it," I lied. "He's really not as bad as you and Ally think."

"Sure, sure, whatever you say," Cindy rolled her eyes and gestured to the cab driver to continue to the party destination. She pulled out her lipstick and made some last flourishes to her face before she squealed with excitement that the night was just beginning.

*

We pulled up outside a strip of bars where people were lingering in a long line. Thin plumes of smoke drifted away from the ends of cigarettes, and the air was alive with excited chatter. The people all looked glamorous and I suddenly felt underdressed, although when I expressed this concern Cindy was quick to tell me that I looked great. She also pointed out the few lingering looks I was getting from men as evidence of this. I rubbed the back of my neck and dipped my head to ensure that I would not meet their gaze as I wasn't used to this type of attention.

"You know it's a shame that you're still with Mark. A night like this is a great way to meet someone. You know, you just dance and smile and let your body do the talking and then suddenly... bam, you're right in the heat of the moment and everything is just wonderful," Cindy smiled and swayed, as though she was lost in a hazy memory.

"Yes, well, I am with Mark," I said. Cindy shot me a look and arched an eyebrow, but she didn't say anything further. Cindy linked arms with me and flashed a smile at the people we passed in the line. They frowned, wondering why we were so special when they had to wait. We approached the bouncers.

"Hey handsome," Cindy said with a sultry smile, and promptly gave our names. I had never been important enough to attend an event like this so I assumed that there was going to be some mistake and they weren't going to let me in, but they opened the rope barrier and ushered us through, much to the consternation of the people behind us. But their groans were not my concern as I stepped into a wonderland of lights and music. The air pounded with a steady rhythm and strobe lights flashed around a dark room. People swarmed around the bar and clustered in groups. I felt an excited tingle, as though I was absorbing all the vibrant energy in the air, and started to move to the music.

"Let's go and see Blake," Cindy said, dragging me across the dance floor towards the DJ booth. Blake was a tall white guy with dusty blonde hair. He nodded along to the music. Headphones were slung around his neck and he wore a long white t-shirt. Cindy called out to him. I was struck by his boyish charm and the danger that lurked within his eyes. Perhaps Cindy was right and this was a place for me to rediscover myself, although it wouldn't be with Blake. I could see from the way Cindy looked at him that she had eyes for him. He smiled and nodded back, although it was difficult to discern if he had as much interest in her as she had in him. She introduced me and he asked me if I wanted a particular song played during the night. I thanked him for getting us on the list.

"Anything for Cindy," he said. We giggled as we moved towards the bar, eager to begin our night of drinking.

"So, you and Blake huh?" I asked as we nestled into a corner, sipping on the icy alcohol, letting it linger inside and take hold of our bodies.

Cindy nodded, her body swaying to the music. We leaned into each other, but still had to yell in order for us to hear each other. "Not yet, but I'm hoping. I've been crushing on him for ages now and I just want things to happen. The problem is that he always DJ's at these things, he never just enjoys them. I can't dance with him in the booth."

"I'm sure he might let you if you asked him nicely," I replied.

"Yeah, maybe," Cindy nodded. "So what's it like being in a long term relationship? I mean, aren't you ever tempted when there are so many hot guys around?" she cast a glance around the nearby vicinity and indeed there were a number of handsome men hovering around us. Not that any of them caught my eye, although deep inside there was a flicker as I remembered my hands sliding along Jack's body, feeling the contours of his flesh and the hard angles of his muscles. I was glad that the lights were low so the blush on my cheeks was hidden.

"I mean, you know, sure sometimes you can fall into a routine and things aren't exactly wild, but that's worth the trade off. I mean, I have stability. I can rely on Mark. I know that he's not going anywhere and I know that he's not going to leave."

I know that he's not going to let me leave either, I thought. I shuddered a little at the prospect of being a prisoner to him, a slave to his devotion without any hope of escape. And what of a child? What life would they know? God forbid they should suffer as I had suffered, but worse... what if they turned out be just like him?

I tried to quell the uneasy feelings that slithered inside me because I wanted one night where I didn't have to think about these things, one night when I could be an ordinary person without all this emotional baggage.

"Well, it sounds pretty great I guess. I get tired of coming home to an empty apartment," Cindy said. "But then again sometimes it is fun to flirt and dance." Despite her attraction to Blake, Cindy didn't seem to have any qualms about enjoying the dancing company of other men. She quickly caught the eye of one guy and elegantly joined him on the dance floor, their bodies moving in harmony. I nursed my drink and watched proceedings. A guy came up to me and asked to buy me a drink, but I declined, saying that I had a boyfriend. As I watched Cindy envy rose within me though. She lived a life of freedom and wasn't defined by worry and fear. She laughed and drifted between men, unafraid of disappointing them because she knew that this was just fun, and her real feelings were set on Blake.

Eventually she came back to me and tried to pull me onto the dance floor.

"Come on Sandi. I brought you here to have a good time! This is a girl's night out, you can't just stand on the sidelines. Let your hair down."

"I really don't think that's a good idea, I mean, I want to, but there are a lot of guys here and Mark would be upset."

"Oh, you need to stop thinking about what Mark wants and act on what you want. He's not here anyway, and it's not like you're going to do anything. There's nothing wrong with a little bit of dancing, and if the guy wants too much then you just walk away and dance somewhere else. Come on, you know you won't regret it."

This time when she tugged at my arms I did not resist. There was something inside me that wanted to be a part of this world, something that I couldn't ignore. For so long I had kept myself restrained for Mark's sake. I had controlled myself and ensured that I wouldn't do anything he disapproved of because I kept telling myself that we were in a relationship and compromises had to be made. Yet it always felt like I was the one making the compromises. Why shouldn't I dance? I knew I wasn't going to be unfaithful to him. I knew that I wasn't going to jeopardize our relationship because that was more important to me than some dance could ever be. But why couldn't he see that? Why did he seem so convinced that I was going to let him down?

Well I wasn't going to allow myself to be in thrall to him on this occasion. This was my night to enjoy with Cindy, and I couldn't resist the urge to dance. We slipped into the undulating crowd, surrendering our bodies to the rhythm alongside everyone else. We laughed and stayed close to each other as I felt the heat of other people surging around us. Sweat prickled on my body and trickled down. The strobe lighting illuminated me for an instant, and then plunged me into darkness. My limbs swayed, my hair matted to my face, and the relentless rhythm of the music tore through my body and took over from the natural rhythm of my heartbeat. I smiled at Cindy as I felt someone pressing their body against mine. It didn't matter who he was. This was one moment, one instance in time. The fact that I would never speak to him or never see his face made it even more magical, almost like the moment with Jack. I knew I was never going to see him again, and perhaps that made it okay to think about it. After all, it was human nature to think about what might happen under different circumstances. As I danced I let my mind wander, thinking about what might have happened in a different world where I wasn't with Mark. Would I have resisted temptation and acted like I had before, showing Jack out? Or would I have embraced the wild side that lived deep inside me and taken a chance, even though it was strictly against the rules of the job.

My thoughts swirled inside me, carried by the music. I imagined what it would have been like to reach out and touch him in that final place, to feel the last ounce of tension leave his body in a warm stream. I felt warmer than before, but it was good to remember what it was like to desire something. Part of me worried that I had lost the ability to be sexual and sensual. Between Mark and I, sex had become a chore, a routine. He wanted it, so I gave it to him because it at least mollified his temper and decreased his levels of aggression. But there was rarely any tenderness to it. It was a bestial, primal act, one fueled by a biological compulsion rather than any yearning of the soul.

Hands slipped around my waist and tried to pull me closer. Panic flared inside me and thoughts of Jack vanished. I jerked myself away, suddenly worried that somehow Mark would know. I twisted into space and tried to keep a smile on my face, but I could feel bodies everywhere and I wondered how there could be so damned many of them. Light flashed and I gazed through the crowd, the sea of faces blurring into each other, but there was one that stood out from the rest and I couldn't believe it was him. Through everyone else I saw him; Jack, standing there as plain as day. My mouth hung open and I blinked, and then he was gone.

It must have been a trick of the mind. I must have had too much to drink. I pushed myself through the crowd and retreated to the restroom, where I took a few moments to compose myself. There was a group of girls in there, gossiping and talking about which guy they were going to leave with. How easy it was for them to be carefree, and how wonderful it must have been to have that many friends. I gulped in air and paced across the floor until I was ready to return. I, of course, dismissed the idea that I had actually seen Jack from my mind, although it was worrying that I had conjured such a powerful image of him. I had to try and stop myself from thinking about him because Mark would know. I didn't know how, but somehow he would know.

I opened my purse and rummaged around for some tissue to dab the sweat from my brow. I laughed as I caught a somber reflection of myself in the mirror. Drenched in sweat with hair matted in thick strands I didn't think I made a very appealing sight, so Mark didn't have anything to worry about at all. I quickly checked my phone, just in case there was an emergency. My heart sank when I saw that I had about forty missed calls, all of them from Mark. He must have been ringing me constantly and I had been oblivious. But as well as calling me he had sent me texts as well, and the last one gave me chills.

Come outside, it read. My throat dried and as I made my way back to Cindy there was great trepidation in my heart.

Chapter Nine

Cindy's petite frame was in the middle of a cluster of guys. She had one hand clamped on her scalp and twisted her body, while the men watched on in awe and adoration. If I had been in more of a generous mood I would have pitied them, for none of them stood a chance at achieving their hopes. They were merely ways to pass the time until Cindy could be with Blake. I barged through the crowd and made my way to Cindy, wondering what I should do. She looked up. The guys around me groaned and scowled, but I didn't care. Cindy noticed the panicked look on my face. I showed her my phone, and the curse word she said was drowned out by the music. We retreated from the dance floor and huddled together near the wall. I scrolled through my phone and showed her how busy Mark had been.

"What the hell is he thinking? Do you think he actually is outside?" Cindy asked.

"I wouldn't put it past him."

"But why? Can he really not handle you being out for one night?"

I looked despondent. "He says he worries about me and he doesn't trust me being in places like this."

Cindy's mouth dropped open. She placed a hand on my shoulder. "Sandi, you know that this isn't right, right? You shouldn't be treated like this. He's not your parent and you're not some kid who doesn't know any better. You're an adult and you can make your own decisions. He can't expect to treat you like this. Is he like this all the time?"

I shrugged. "Mostly," I said. The effect of the alcohol had worn off. The music gave me a headache. I had been able to lose myself in the excitement of the night up until looking at my phone. It was as though he had poured cold water all over me.

"Sandi," Cindy tilted her head. I hated the look on her face. I had seen it plenty of times before. It was the look the adults at the orphanage gave me whenever I was passed over for another kid. It was in Patrick's eyes as he told me that he didn't know me. It was in my eyes every time I looked at my own reflection. "You shouldn't have to live like this. This isn't normal. You do know that right?"

I nodded silently. Of course I knew, but that didn't make it any easier to cope with. What was I supposed to do instead, just kick Mark to the sidewalk and then enjoy life by myself again? Sure, that had gone great so far.

"I know he's not perfect, but-"

"Not perfect?! Sandi, come on, this is proper psycho behavior. I would never let anyone treat me like this. You have to get out of there before it's too late. I've watched too many crimes shows not to know how this ends," Cindy said, her words forceful and aggressive. Her reaction was more powerful than I had imagined and it made me wonder if I had let things get too far, made too many excuses for Mark's behavior. It was easy to justify things and rationalize things. Sometimes it took another person to make you truly see what was happening. Then my phone buzzed again. Mark was calling me. Again. Then another text pinged through.

I know you're in there. Come outside. I just want to talk to you for a minute.

Cindy grabbed my arm. "You don't have to go out there Sandi. Don't give in to his demands. Just stay here and enjoy yourself. This is our night. Don't let him ruin it."

But he had already ruined it. How could I simply put my phone away and ignore it when I knew that it would be going off? How could I enjoy myself when I knew he was outside? I shook my head and tucked my phone into my purse.

"I'll be back in a minute," I said. "I'm just going to talk to him and then he'll leave. I know he will," I added with unjustified certainty. The disapproving look on Cindy's face was burned into my mind. I knew what she was thinking; that I was a victim and that I was hopeless, but I could make him leave and then I could get back to enjoying the night.

*

I walked outside and I walked into a wall of cold air. The sweat evaporated off my skin and I shivered.

"Why the hell aren't you letting me in? I'm telling you that I know someone in there and I'm only going to be a minute. God, she's my fiancée! Don't you have a heart? I just want to say something to her and then I'll be out," Mark said. He paced around a small patch of grass between the entrance to this venue and the road. Smokers were gathered, watching on with interest at this stranger trying to convince the bouncer to let him in. Other people were still queuing, shuddering and huddling together to brace themselves against the chill of the night. The bouncer was resolute, standing stoically with his hands clasped in front of him.

"And I'm telling you that if you're not on the list then you have to get to the back of the line," he said, gesturing to the snaking line that curved around the building.

"I don't have time for that! My fiancée is in there and she's not answering my phone calls. I'm worried that something has happened to her," Mark said desperately. The bouncer shrugged and remained silent. Mark's eyes narrowed. I worried that he was going to do something he was going to regret later. It was always hard to keep a lid on his anger and I could see the veins throbbing on his forehead. I skipped past the bouncer, making myself visible through the crowd, and the relief on his face when he saw me was palpable.

"Oh baby, I've been so worried about you!" he cried, rushing towards me. I wasn't blind to the fact that the people around us were using us as a piece of amusement. I also remembered what Cindy had said, about how I didn't have to live with this. I knew she was right. The sense of freedom that I had enjoyed from being out here had vanished completely. Now it was replaced by a revolting nauseous feeling in the pit of my stomach, and I definitely knew that that should not have been the feeling greeting me when I saw my fiancé. I was determined to be strong and to resolve myself against weakening against him.

"What are you doing here Mark?"

He stood there with his hands reaching out to me. There was an imploring look on his face, and for a moment I could have actually believed that his emotions were sincere. But that was Mark's greatest trick. He could slip masks on easily, one after the other, but deep down the only thing that bothered him was anything that threatened to take away his control.

"What do you mean? I think it's obvious," he said. "Look, I know I acted like an ass before about this whole night and I just wanted to come and say that I'm sorry. I didn't want your night to be ruined by any drama that's happening at home. I just wanted to come here and get it all out in the open and tell you that I'm sorry. I don't want to be the kind of guy that makes you feel guilty for wanting to enjoy yourself. I was out of line and I shouldn't have made such a big stink about it."

I tilted my head and looked at him, wondering for a moment if he really meant what he said. But, damn it, I wanted to believe him. I wanted to give him chance after chance after chance, so I walked towards him and took his hands. Perhaps this was the shock to the system he needed. Maybe this was the turning point for us, and all of a sudden I felt silly for being so negative about him. Mark's love manifested itself in a different way to the love of other people. It was aggressive and severe, but that didn't mean it was any less valid than other types of love and I just had to adjust to that.

"Mark, I really appreciate you saying that, and I know it's a grand gesture, but you really didn't need to come down here and say this. It could have waited until I came home."

His eye twitched and I could tell that he was making a concerted effort to keep his voice steady. "I thought it would be romantic and I wanted you to understand how sorry I am. I just wanted to take the weight off your mind and let you know that I'm not going to be like that any longer."

"Okay Mark, I appreciate that, I really do, so are you going to be okay getting home now and we can talk about this again later?" I felt like every word was liable to make him explode, and I said each one with trepidation.

"Well, I thought that since I'm here you could take me in with you. The bouncer is being an ass."

"Yeah, I mean, that's not really how it works though. I'm a guest myself so I don't think I can get anyone on the list, and this was supposed to be a girl's night out with Cindy."

"I know, but you are engaged, and I did come all the way down here to make this grand romantic gesture. I think the least you can do is this for me," he said. "And if you can't get me in then how about we just go home and have a nice cozy night? We can light some candles and enjoy making up," he slipped his arm around my shoulders surreptitiously, but I pulled away. I wasn't going to let him get away with this.

"Mark, no," I said, loud and clear. The sharp words cut through the chill night sky. A crowd had begun to gather as people realized that something out of the ordinary was happening outside. There was nothing like the drama of a couple on the rocks to get people interested. "You can't just come here and expect me to come home with you. I told you that I'm going to be out tonight, and the night isn't over yet. I appreciate you coming out here to tell me that you're sorry and I thank you for it, but that doesn't just mean you get what you want in the end. I'm staying here with Cindy. You should go home. I promise we'll talk about this more when I get back."

I spoke as firmly as I could and stepped back, trying to move away from him, but he was always so quick with his movements. He grabbed my arm, his fingers digging deep in my flesh. Pain bloomed and I winced.

"You're hurting me," I gasped, but he didn't care.

"I come out here being all nice and apologetic and this is how you treat me? My God you are an ungrateful bitch. Sometimes I don't know why I bother. And why do you want me to go so badly, huh? Are you having too much fun in there? Dancing along like the little slut you are? Don't pretend like you haven't been enjoying yourself. I can smell them on you," he sneered. I was still gasping, trying to wrench my arm free, but his grip was too tight. It always was.

"I haven't done anything Mark!"

"Don't lie to me. I know you think I'm a joke and you're just coming out here to let off some steam. I should never have allowed you to come to a place like this. I knew the temptation would be too much. It's time to go home Sandi."

He started to drag me away. I cried out and tried to pull myself free, but it wasn't working.

"Somebody help her!" a shrill voice cried. I thought it was Cindy's.

"Aren't you going to do something," another angry voice said. This one sounded familiar as well, although I was in too much of a frenzy to try and place it. Mark scowled, his face twisting into something ugly and I knew that he was going to take out the rest of his temper on me when we got home. His apology had been hollow. It had all been a ploy to get me away from the club so that he could get his hands on me again and sink his controlling claws into me. Hair fell across my face as I twisted and writhed, but his strength was such that he dragged me away like a little ragdoll. Perhaps that was all I was. After all, no real family had ever wanted me. I was always left on the shelf. Only Mark had seen fit to claim me and maybe he was right to use me as he saw fit.

It wasn't as though anyone else cared.

Then, suddenly, out of nowhere there was a burst of movement. A dark shadow rushed past the corner of my eye and came slamming into Mark. Pain throbbed on my arm where he had gripped me, and now that he wasn't dragging me any longer I slumped to the grass. The two men rolled. Mark cursed and fought back, but the other man blocked him and jabbed him in the gut. He grabbed Mark's shoulders and threw him out into the road, as though he was just some trash. Mark sprawled out, spitting blood as he pushed himself to his feet, while a crowd of well-meaning onlookers walked up to him.

In the meantime the mysterious savior turned to face me and asked me if I was okay. I nodded, amazed that it was Jack.

Chapter Ten

"Come on, let's get you out of here," Jack said, wrapping his jacket around me. Suddenly I was surrounded by the scent of him as he pulled me up. My legs were shaking as he escorted me away. Everything else was a blur around me. I heard Jack curse at the bouncer, who merely replied that his job was to guard the door and that we hadn't been near the door. I didn't know where Jack was taking me, but I was too shaken to resist. Mark had never lost control like that, not in public. Had he become too complacent or was he finally starting to snap? Jack pushed me into a car and we drove away. My heart thumped. It was erratic, as though it was still following the beat of the music Blake had played. The lights of the city blurred by, as though it was melting around me.

"Are you okay?" Jack asked. "I'm going to take you somewhere safe, away from that maniac," he said. I nodded, unable to bring myself to form words. I felt humiliated that my deep dark secret was out there for the world to see.

Eventually we pulled up to a tall building, one of those that I always passed and wondered who lived inside. There was a security guard who nodded when he saw Jack. We ascended the tower in a silent elevator, which reached a penthouse suite overlooking the entire city.

"Make yourself comfortable. I'll get you some chai tea, for your nerves. Would you like anything to eat?" he asked.

I shook my head and stumbled my way to the couch. He had an open plan kitchen and turned his back to me as he brewed tea. A plush leather couch sat in the middle of the room, and a coffee table was beside it, upon which sat a laptop. There was no TV, but against one wall was a crammed bookshelf. Dotted around the room were various ornaments of abstract art. At first I was amazed that no TV was present, but then I looked out at the view and realized that he simply didn't need one. We were up high enough that we could escape the light pollution of the city. Thin clouds were visible, as was the full, sensual moon. The night was a dark cloak that shrouded the world and there was something about being so close to it, as though I could simply hop outside and leap to the moon, then dance among the stars.

Or perhaps I just liked it because it was far away from Mark.

He came back with a mug of tea. I clasped it in two hands. The weight of his jacket was still around my shoulders, although I didn't want to take it off because I was wearing something revealing and it seemed wrong to wear such a thing in his home. His jacket was imbued with the scent of his musky aftershave. It was similar to what I had sensed when giving him a massage, although then it had been a whisper in among the other fragrances of my massage parlor. I tried not to gawk at the penthouse suite, but it was difficult to not marvel at it. I couldn't imagine how much it cost to live here, and it made me wonder what Jack did for a living. Who was this man that could afford to live among the clouds?

The tea was calming and warm. I had stopped shivering by now. Jack had poured himself a cup as well, and came to join me on the couch, although he sat at the opposite end, leaving sensible distance between us. My gaze flickered toward and away from him, never settling on any one area. This was a man whose flesh I had massaged, a man who I had seen every inch of, and the memory of it still caused a flame to flicker within my heart. I sipped the tea, unable to forget his manhood in all its impressive stature. How was it possible that he was there when I needed him most?

"I have to admit I wasn't expecting to see you there. Do you always have this much trouble with your boyfriend?" Jack asked.

I cringed, wishing that the ground would swallow me up. It would have been easier had I never gone out with Cindy, although I tried not to think like that because that's exactly what Mark would have wanted.

"Not all the time he just... he didn't like me going out clubbing. He was afraid that some guy would take advantage of me I guess."

"Then he would really hate knowing you're here with me," Jack said. He wore a half-smirk, although I couldn't tell if he was joking or not. I had been used to speaking with him having his face turned away from me. There was a kind of safety that came with the massage parlor. While the men were naked and I had my hands on them I was in control. I was the one who could guide the conversation. It was my domain, and I never had to feel unsettled or alone. But now I was in his home, and I felt entirely uneasy with my position here. I didn't know what I should do or say. I didn't even know what he wanted with me. There was a deep intensity radiating from his body. It played havoc with my mind. My breaths were slow and long. I eventually managed to calm my heart.

"Probably," I said, my voice numb and hollow. Jack frowned and pressed his lips together.

"Look, I don't mean to pry," he began, but I cut him off.

"Then don't," I said. Really it was none of his business. We were just strangers who happened to be thrown together due to circumstance. And yet there was a gnawing feeling in the back of my mind that it might have been more than that.

"Why were you there anyway?" I asked, trying to steer the conversation away from my own circumstances. For a moment I thought Jack was going to fight me and try and get me to talk about what had happened, but he gave me the dignity of answering my question.

"I was there for the party of course, although I don't remember you being at the dinner."

"The dinner?"

"To honor Margaret Smythe. That was the whole point of the evening, although it seems her nephew didn't take his aunt into account when he arranged the evening's entertainment. I can't imagine that nightclub ever appealing to her. The dinner was a dignified thing though, although I didn't see you there."

"Oh, I don't know anything about the dinner or this Smythe person," I said, laughing nervously, "I was just there with my friend Cindy. She knew the DJ and got us in. I should message her actually," I said, reaching into my purse for my phone. I scrolled past the endless messages from Mark. They ranged from apologetic to angry, covering the entire spectrum of emotion and they just blurred into one as I sent Cindy a text telling her that I was safe and she didn't need to worry about me. I slipped my phone back in my purse and swallowed a lump in my throat, ashamed at the way Mark was acting.

"I see, well, I hope you were enjoying yourself up until your boyfriend showed up."

It was then I realized that I hadn't thanked him. "Jack, thanks for what you did. I know you didn't have to. It would have been alright in the end anyway, but thank you all the same."

"How is your arm?" he asked.

I twisted my neck and saw the ugly bruise, the sickly shade of yellow mixing with the dark purplish swamp. "It's fine," I said.

"Does this happen often?" Jack asked gently.

"I don't want to talk about my private life," I said, placing my tea on the coffee table. I rose from the couch and strode towards the window, looking down on the city below. There were other skyscrapers, twins of this tower. At this time of night the windows were dark, and only faint flickers of movement could be seen. I hated the way he thought he could just pry into my life because he had seen me at my worst, or because he thought we shared some connection because I had seen him naked. We weren't special. He was just a guy, and I didn't have to tell him anything.

"What do you do to afford this?" I asked.

Jack chuckled as he came to stand beside me. His towering form reminded me of a skyscraper, firm and rigid, carved to withstand anything that might come its way. I couldn't imagine even a tornado ripping Jack's roots from where he stood. He had the kind of inner steel that I had always envied. I doubted that anyone would treat him in a way that he wouldn't approve of.

"Do you really not know who I am?" he asked.

I looked at him and shrugged.

He sighed. "I suppose it's my own fault for trying to be reclusive. I've never been one to open myself up to the public. The marketing department would have a coronary though. They're always telling me that I should put a face to the company, that people want to see the person behind the brand," he shook his head and laughed gently. "I'm Jack Easter. I own the Easter Corporation, which in turn owns other brands," and he listed off a lot of companies, some of them I had even heard of.

"So, you're one of those rich guys that pulls the strings of the world?" I asked flippantly. It unnerved me when he only flashed me a smirk.

"I wouldn't go that far, but I try and use my wealth for good. My great-grandfather was the one who started the business, and since then it's gone from strength to strength."

"And one day your son is going to take over from you? That's quite a legacy."

I saw something flash across his face, although I wasn't quite sure what it was. He glanced down at his tea and he licked his lips.

"I don't have a son yet," he said.

"I don't either. Sometimes I wonder whether it's right to bring a child into the world when there's so much strife and uncertainty about the future. I mean, what birthright am I really giving to them? And then there's-" I was about to say 'Mark,' but I managed to stop myself. I tore my gaze nervously away from Jack, and was glad when he didn't press the matter.

"I suppose it's something we all have to think about, but then if everyone decided that the world was too dangerous then the human race would go extinct. The only way we can truly be sure the world will be a better place is if we raise responsible children to take care of it. Anyway, things are a lot better now than they have been at other points in history."

"I guess," I said, although I still felt as though I had a responsibility to the child of mine that hadn't been born yet. "So what do you, like, do with your time? I mean, do you just hand off everything to your subordinates and let your money work for yourself?"

"I wish," Jack smirked. "We Easter boys have always had a strong work ethic. If we didn't work hard then the company wouldn't be where it is today, and if I took my foot off the gas then it would slowly start to crumble. I'm not going to become complacent just because we've been a success. I have a strict routine, as I want to set an example to everyone who works for us."

"Sounds like you put a lot of pressure on yourself," I said.

"Pressure is what makes life worthwhile. You have to test yourself, otherwise you won't know where your limits lie."

"Is that really what you do with your time? Work?"

"What else is there?" Jack asked, frowning. I looked at him with disbelief.

"Jack, you're what, a millionaire?" He raised his eyebrows, indicating that I should go higher. "Billionaire then," I said, and this time he smiled. "And all you can think to do with your time is to work. You have enough money in the world to do anything you want. God... if I had that money I'd... I'd... I don't know! There's too much choice! I can barely scrape a few dollars together and here you are with the means to do anything and you're just wasting it!" I gestured with my arms and gazed at him, astounded because to me it seemed like he had the golden ticket to life, but he hadn't cashed it in. Why would he work when the world was out there waiting for him to explore?

He arched an eyebrow. "And what would you do if you had the luxury of wealth?"

"I don't know..." I thought for a moment as he waited for me to answer. "I guess I'd go traveling I mean, there's plenty of places that I'd like to see, both here and abroad. I'd get myself a whole new wardrobe, and a new place that has enough space for everything I need. I'd maybe take some cooking lessons or try my hand at art." I struggled to think of anything extravagant to use the money for. Patrick and I used to speak about what we'd do if we were ever adopted by rich people. Back then it had been easy to think of things, like buying an elephant or having an ice sculpture made of ourselves. It struck me how mundane my dreams had become, and I wondered how much of myself had I lost over the years?

"Okay, so maybe they're not the most exciting things," I added, "but I'm sure I could think of more. It'd just be nice to not worry about bills and things for a while. I'd like to enjoy life without feeling like I owe someone something. It'd just be nice to have the weight taken off my shoulders for a while." My tone turned more despondent as we talked. Jack nodded silently. I gazed out of the window, looking at the ghosts of our reflections staring back at us. I wondered if there was ever a path of life I could have taken that would lead me to live a luxurious life like this, or if I was always meant to struggle.

The moments ticked by and I suddenly wondered what I was doing there with Jack, and where this night was going to lead. He had rescued me for the night, but it wasn't as though I could just leave my life behind. Mark would be waiting for me at home. I didn't have enough money to begin somewhere new. I shrugged off his jacket and placed it on the couch.

"I should be going," I said weakly. Jack turned to face me.

"Do you have somewhere else to stay?" he asked. I shook my head. I suppose that I could have asked Cindy or Ally for refuge, but that almost felt like accepting defeat, or just prolonging the inevitable. "Sandi, I'm not going to pry because I know you want to keep your business to yourself, but why are you with him?"

There were so many ways I could have answered that particular question, for some reason I decided to tell him the truth. Perhaps it was because I knew I would never see him again so there was no danger, or it might have been because I just wanted the freedom of being able to speak without being afraid of how people might react.

"Because I don't want to be alone."

I know some people will think I'm a coward for saying that, and maybe I am, but the world is a scary and cruel place when you have nobody to stand beside you. It was bad enough at the orphanage, but then when I was released it was even worse. There are people all around living their own lives, and yet it feels like you're distant from them, stranded or forgotten in this abyss and nobody bothers to reach out. They walk by. Perhaps they offer a pitiful glance, but mostly they just look through you and you might as well not exist at all. Mark wasn't perfect, but at least when I was with him I didn't have to fear being forgotten or fading away from the world. At least I mattered to someone.

I wasn't going to wait for Jack to judge me. I was grateful for him bringing me here, but I knew it was a mistake. We were from different paths and while our paths had crossed there was nothing tying us together. At least I thought not. But then he said something extremely surprising.

He looked at me in a way that few had looked at me before. His intense gaze peeled away my brittle layers, and I squirmed under the force of the sensations. Up here in his tower we were away from the world, away from everything. There was a sense of unpredictability and magic, as though anything might happen.

"What if I could change that for you?" he asked. His voice was as smooth as silk. A tingle ran down my spine, and the fine hairs on the back of my neck stood on end. His handsomeness was beguiling. His eyes were dark and mysterious, two pools that led to somewhere fraught with danger. He was devilishly handsome, and like the devil

I wondered if he would enchant me with his dark ways. This was his domain, and I was utterly vulnerable to him.

"What do you mean?" I asked, my voice trembling.

"I mean that I could find a way to give you some financial freedom."

"What, like a donation?" I asked, indignant at the thought that I would be treated like some charity.

"Not a donation. For services rendered."

"What kind of services?"

He parted his lips and stroked his jaw. His collar was open. I remembered how taut his shoulders were, how warm his skin had been. "I'm going to be honest with you Sandi; my routine is rigorous and I don't have time for human connection. Frankly I meet few people who can capture my attention for more than a few moments, but you are one of them. I sympathize with your plight and I don't like the thought of you going back to a man who treats you like that. If you truly feel trapped then we can come to an arrangement. I am not in the habit of giving money away. You have created an impression in my mind, and I find that I am unable to stop thinking about you. I am most unused to feeling this way."

"What are you proposing Jack?" I asked warily, afraid of where this conversation was going. He was sure taking his time getting to the point, and that meant it was likely something that I was not going to like to hear.

"One night Sandi. That's all I ask. One night with you and I'll make sure that you never have to depend on anyone else again. You'll have your freedom, and I'll have my happy ending."

My stomach turned as he said this. My mind was flushed with all kinds of thoughts. At first I was horrified that he would treat me this way. Mark had always said I was one step away from being a common whore, but the amount of money Jack could afford... I hated myself for even considering it, but I couldn't dismiss it out of hand. Was surrendering my body for one night really such a big price to pay for a lifetime of freedom?

"You don't have to make a decision now. Take my card. Call me," he said, placing a card in my hand. Our palms met and I felt a surge of fire spread through my arm. I nodded and turned away from him. He told me that his driver would take me back home, and he was insistent that he could change my life.

I left his tower then. He had been my savior once, was this him trying to save me again, or was he just trying to take advantage of a broken woman? Billionaires like him didn't have the best reputation. They played with people like me, treating us like toys because they were bored. But even so I tucked the card inside my purse and gnawed on my lower lip, wondering what the hell I was going to do next.

Chapter Eleven

The house was a foreboding fortress. It had been my home for a long time. It had my touches inside, although never as many as I wanted because Mark always cried foul that he wasn't allowed to leave his impression on the place, although his consisted of bikes and babes and tacky displays of machismo. The windows were dark. The neighborhood was quiet. Unlike the pristine, modern buildings in the city this suburb was rundown. Lawns were patchy and overgrown. Metal fences kept wild dogs away from pedestrians. The houses were paint-flecked and drab, with patio doors creaking as they swung, begging to be torn off and put out of their misery. Fences were slanted, forever downed by a storm. Down the street an old car had been abandoned. Nobody knew whose it was, and it had been there for so long that nobody questioned it. When there was nothing else to compare it to I could almost convince myself that this place had its charm, but in reality it was a nightmare. I could dress it up as much as I wanted, but when compared to the striking tower that Jack occupied it fell well short of being acceptable. It was my prison, soaking up rent, preventing me from saving to move anywhere else. And inside was a monster, tethering myself to him because my fear anchored me here.

I turned to look out at the street stretching out either side of me, disappearing into the darkness. I might well have started walking in either direction, but I knew that neither way would lead me to anywhere better because there was nowhere better. There was only here, and I had to try and make the best of it. I had to confront the monster.

I walked in. Shadows fell through the house. Slivers of moonlight broke through the darkness.

"You're home," Mark said in a dry, drawling voice. I moved into the lounge and saw his silhouette on the couch. He leaned forward with his hands clasped together, resting his chin on his knuckles. "I wasn't sure you'd come back."

"Of course I came back. This is my home," I said.

"I thought you had gone off with him. Who is he? Did you meet him tonight? Is that why you didn't want me to come into the club?"

"He's just some guy Mark. It's not important who he is."

"Great. So I'm losing you to someone who isn't even important. This is exactly what I was afraid of Sandi. Don't you see this? It's all coming true. I told you that I didn't want you to go out to places like this. They're designed to tempt women away from their men. It's a story as old as time. I thought I'd done enough to keep you here. I've given you a nice place to live. I work every day to make sure there's food on the table, and I even let you work at your job," he sneered as he spoke about her work. "Why aren't you happy here?"

I couldn't believe that he was actually asking the question. Was the answer really not evident? I needed to be here, with him, now, in order to put this all to rest. I had put up with it for too long.

"Because you hit me Mark. Because you make me feel like crap. You're suspicious even when you have no reason to be. You shout at me and act as though I'm betraying you every day when all I'm doing is working. You get angry, so damned angry at the slightest provocation. I can't have an honest conversation with you because you never listen to me. You just jump to conclusions and expect the worst, and then you make these hollow attempts to make things better, but all you're doing is papering over the cracks. You keep telling me that you're going to change, but you never do. You just put on an act to get what you want and then things go back to normal. And for a time I could put up with all of that because I didn't have anything else to hope for, but now life is moving on and we're getting closer to the future and we're talking about children. I just... I can't allow someone else to come into our lives. Not when you're like this. Not when you take out your anger at the world on me. It's not fair Mark, and if you can't see that then I don't know what you expect of me."

Once the words started they flowed out without stopping. It was as though the floodgates had been opened. I was able to be honest with him in a way that I hadn't been before, but suddenly my fear had evaporated. There was no reason to hold anything back any longer. My words were quiet, and yet they carried with them the force of my entire heart. I stood in the doorway of the lounge, ready to make a hasty retreat as I expected Mark to explode with anger as he had done so many times before. But, instead, he slumped down as though he was a puppet and his strings had been cut.

"I just don't know what to do," Mark said. "I try you know, I really try. I know that I've treated you badly and I shouldn't hit you, but sometimes I just get so mad. I don't know what comes over me and I can't control myself. I keep wanting to be better. I tell myself that I'm going to be better, but then it happens again. I just want things to be the way they are in my head. You shouldn't have to work as a masseuse. I should be able to provide for you."

"Things can't be like they are in your head Mark. The world doesn't work that way. And you might think that my job isn't worthwhile, but I happen to like it. I'm good at what I do and it brings me pride to know that I'm valued by the people I work with, and that I can make people's lives a little better. You can't control everyone around you. We're not toy soldiers."

"I know you're not, I just... I just wish things were different. You're the best thing that's ever happened to me and I don't want to lose you. When I saw you that night in the bar I fell in love with you immediately. I knew that I had to have you. I swore to myself that I was never going to let you go."

His words were tinged with sorrow. I thought back to that night as well. It was the day I had reunited with Patrick, and had been shunned. I staggered into a bar seeking to drown my sorrows, wondering what could have happened to Patrick to make him act like that. I thought about the past, and how the love we had shared with each other had likely been a lie. I felt like such a fool. Perhaps the only good thing I had ever nurtured in the world had died that day, and I didn't think anything would ever be able to replace it. I was sullen and brash when Mark came up to me. He sat beside me, ignoring my disapproving grunts. He ordered drink after drink. At first he tried to engage me in conversation, and then he sat in silence. He poured money into the jukebox, trying to find a song that made me smile. Eventually he succeeded. It hadn't all been bad. That first night was promising. I started to think that maybe I just had to let go of the past, to cut all ties and stride into the future. As the hours dragged , the bar became empty but the drinks kept coming. I was impressed by his persistence. Few people had ever stayed around me this long. He bothered with me when few else had, so when he asked me for a dance at the end of the night I felt like I had to oblige him. I guess that summed our relationship up really. I felt indebted to him so he took what he wanted. We danced in the empty bar as the bartender cleaned up after all. Our words were slurred and then he kissed me. I kissed him back, filled with anger at Patrick. Maybe in a way I had been the villain all along because I had never loved Mark, not really, not truly. Anger had drawn me to him, and fear kept me with him. Once he had me in his arms I didn't want to leave. I didn't want to feel alone again. I clung to him desperately and I didn't let go; not when he abused me, not when he hit me, not when he yelled... I was there for all of it, but I couldn't let anyone else suffer at his hand. And it was time for me to realize I deserved better.

"I can't stay just because you want me to," I said. "That's not how life works."

"What about if I promise to make things better? What if I promise to work on myself? I can change Sandi, I really can."

"I know you might think that, but you've promised that before."

"I mean it this time!"

I closed my eyes, hardening my heart against his pleas and my own fear of being alone. "You can change for someone else, for the next girl who comes along. I might be the love of your life Mark, but you're not the love of mine. I should have left a long time ago. The things you've been doing... they're not right."

"And where are you going to go?" he asked, his voice tinged with anger.

"I don't know."

"You know you're not going to be the same without me," he said.

I thought back to when Jack had asked me what I would do with all the money in the world. It struck me then that I had lost a lot of myself over the years. There was some excited spark in me that had been doused and I didn't want it to be lost forever. If there was a chance for me to reignite it then I had to change it.

"I hope I'm not Mark," I said. Then I left. I told him that I'd be by another time to collect my things, then I slipped out of the door as though it was the easiest thing in the world.

Chapter Twelve

"I knew that if I stayed there I would never leave. When I walked inside I shuddered and I knew I had to be strong. I thought about what you told me, about how I didn't have to live like this. I think for a long time now I've been stuck in this rut and I haven't been able to see how much of a toll it's been taking on me. I'm sorry for not talking to you properly about it before, and I'm sorry about crashing in on you like this," I said, smiling sheepishly at Cindy.

"You don't have to apologize at all. I'm glad you're here. I'd much rather you come to me than force yourself to stay there for one more night. I can't believe what happened earlier. You're brave Sandi. I don't think I could have gone back in there and faced him alone."

"I guess I'm just used to him hitting me by now," I said. Cindy looked at me forlornly and it was only then that I realized how much I had suffered by Mark's hand. Over the years he had abused me so much that it had normalized things for me. Cindy reached out. As soon as her hands touched me I broke down. Tears streamed down my cheeks and I shuddered terribly, as though my heart broke in that one instant. It felt as though it had been held together by a patchwork of stubbornness and denial, which had now been torn away and all the sorrow flowed out. I fell into Cindy's embrace and she held me tenderly for a long time. I wasn't sure how much time had passed. All the trauma of my life suddenly came surging out and I felt so angry at myself for not having realized this sooner. Why had I punished myself for so long? Why had I stayed with him when I knew that it was bad for me?

Eventually I pulled myself away from Cindy, feeling ashamed. It was rare that I ever showed anyone this side of me.

"I'm sorry," I said.

"You don't have to be sorry," Cindy smiled. "I'm your friend Sandi. I want to help you. I'm just glad you got out of there when you did, and I'm sorry that I didn't do anything sooner. I always suspected that something was up, but I didn't realize it was this bad. I don't know what I'd have done if something horrible happened. You can stay here for as long as you like. I don't want you to go back to him."

"I'm not going to," I said, surprising myself with the determination in my voice. "I feel so stupid now."

"Why?"

"Because I shouldn't have stayed with him for so long."

"It's not your fault. He manipulated you and you were scared. There's no shame in that. It must have been awful to be locked in that world with no way out. I can't imagine it."

"It was. And I just... I'm so afraid of being alone again Cindy. I've been alone all my life and I just can't take it."

"You're not alone Sandi. I'm right here with you." She clasped my hand tightly and smiled at me. Through the shimmering haze of tears I saw her friendly face and I knew that she was right. I wasn't alone. I had been so focused on romantic relationships that I hadn't begun to think about friendships. Despite knowing Cindy for a while I hadn't let her in properly, mostly because I was ashamed of what she might find regarding my relationship with Mark, and now I regretted that. I had put all my hopes and fears onto Mark when there were other people out there, other people like Cindy... and perhaps Jack. I paused for a moment as I thought about his indecent proposal, before I pushed the idea away.

"You should be proud of what you did tonight. People like Mark shouldn't be allowed to get away with this. I couldn't believe what I was seeing when it happened. He just flipped. It was surreal, like watching a movie or something."

"You should try living it," I replied dryly. My arm throbbed with pain, as though thinking about Mark grabbing me made it all the more intense. The ugly bruise was wide and long, coiling around my upper arm. "He's always struggled with anger. Whenever anything doesn't go his way he lashes out. It's as though there's some monster inside him that he can't keep quiet, and when it's out it just goes on a rampage. I should never have let it get this far."

"If you don't mind me asking, why did you?"

I looked up at the ceiling and wiped errant tears from my ears. "I guess I was afraid of being alone. But then we started thinking about the future and the possibility of bringing a child into this world and I just knew that I couldn't condemn anyone to a life with him, and then I started thinking about myself. If I felt that way about a child then why should I be with him? The more I thought about it I realized that I had lost a lot of myself over the years, as though he had been chipping away at me. I thought if I stayed there was going to be nothing left. To be honest I didn't even know I was going to leave him until I stepped into that house. He was sitting there in the darkness and I just felt like a stranger, like I wasn't meant to be there."

"That's good."

"But now it feels as though I've wasted my life." My head dropped and I ran my hand through my hair, pushing it away from my eyes. "I don't know what I'm going to do or who I want to be. I've never known."

Cindy knew a little bit about my past; she knew that I had been in the foster care system and that I had never been adopted. I don't think she understood what a toll that had taken on my identity, but she was sympathetic enough to empathize with me.

"You can do anything you want. You can be anyone you want. That's the beauty of life. And you can stay here until you figure it all out," she said. I hugged her again. "There are always opportunities in this world Sandi, all you have to do is be open to them. I know it's going to take a while for you to get over this, but you will get through it, and you have plenty of years left in your life to find what makes you happy."

I adored Cindy's positivity and in that moment I wanted to believe her with every fiber of my being. However, life had trampled on me so much that I wasn't yet ready to accept hope into my heart.

*

After we spoke for a little while Cindy got some clothes for me and showed me to the guest room, which was currently filled with exercise equipment as Cindy used it as a makeshift gym. I took the opportunity to have a shower, which was welcome as I was still covered in the slick sheen of sweat that had dried on my flesh after a night of dancing. The hot water blasted away my sorrow and the steam rose in a mist around me, enveloping me in this wonderful feeling of being taken away. Right then and there I would have given anything to be transported to another world, to be given another chance at a new beginning. I stayed in there for longer than was normal, as though it was some kind of sanctuary, but eventually I turned the faucet off. Silence reigned around me as the flow of water ceased and the misty steam hung in the air. Water dripped down, trickling along the curves of my body, forming small puddles before it swirled down the gurgling drain. I grabbed a soft towel and wrapped it around me, wincing when I touched the sensitive bruise.

I glanced at the mess of clothes I had peeled away, wondering what might have happened if I had declined Cindy's invitation. Ultimately I decided that it would only have been delaying the inevitable. This night was inexorable, whether it happened now or thirty years from now. There was always going to be a breaking point. I was sorry that I hadn't found it sooner, but glad that I hadn't had to wait any longer. Now that I had broken free of Mark's influence I suddenly saw things in a completely different light. There were no excuses to justify his behavior and I didn't have to make any logical leaps to rationalize it. I could simply accept it for what it was.

I had been abused.

The words were sharp in my mind, like a knife cutting through a veil that made everything hazy. My hands trembled as I picked up the soft, comfortable clothes that Cindy had laid out for me. I covered up my body with them, gnawing on my lower lip. I thought of all the times I could have walked away before. They flashed through my mind's eye, as though illuminated by lightning during a storm. Every time I saw myself I wanted to yell to get out of there before it got worse, but it was as though I was hammering against a glass window, my screams not carrying through the barrier. I groaned as I walked away, rubbing my head. Cindy was waiting for me with a mug of cocoa. The chocolaty aroma filled the room and spoke to something deep inside me; cozy nights as a child, a forbidden treat that always seemed far more delicious because we were never allowed to have it regularly.

"Did you want to stay up and talk for a while, or did you just want to go to bed?" Cindy asked.

My mind was running at a million miles an hour so I knew that even if I lay down in bed I wasn't going to be able to rest. We went back into the lounge, which was decorated with relaxing pictures of tropical idylls, soft colors of cornflower blue and egg white. A vanilla candle burned, mixing with the fragrance of the cocoa wonderfully.

"So, what's the deal with the guy who saved you? I tried to come after you and find you, but you had been whisked away. I was glad when I got your text. I thought that someone had abducted you," Cindy asked. I squirmed a little as I thought about Jack. Every thought of him was laced with this uncertain power that he seemed to command within me.

"He was the same guy who came in for the massage while I was covering your shift; the one that asked for a happy ending."

Cindy's eyebrows rose sharply. "Wow, what the hell was he doing there?"

I shrugged. "He had been invited to the party. Apparently there was some fancy meal beforehand, and then it moved on to the nightclub. I thought I saw him inside, but I had dismissed it because it was too much of a coincidence."

"Well, it's lucky he was there. I think everyone else was too slow to react. You should have seen it afterwards though, that bouncer got chewed out by the management for not doing anything. Everyone else formed this barrier and chased Mark away. I wish he had stuck around so that he could have gotten a taste of his own medicine, but he ran away like a coward. So what's this guy's deal anyway? Where did he take you?"

"Back to his. He gave me some tea and wanted to make sure I was alright. Turns out he's a billionaire. He owns a load of corporations or something."

"Wow. If he comes in again we'll have to charge him a little more,"

I smiled weakly, nodding as I sipped my hot chocolate. "We spoke for a little bit. He's an... interesting man. He doesn't seem to have much going on in his life other than his world. You would have thought that he'd live a wonderful life because of all his money, but it doesn't seem to matter to him."

"Maybe that's why he helped you. Maybe he wanted to feel like a hero for a night."

"Maybe," I replied, but I also wondered if there was something else at play. I shifted uncomfortably. I had never really opened up to anyone about anything, other than Patrick. Even with Mark I had kept my secrets closely guarded inside me. There had been a few girls I called friends who passed through the system, but they were always so temporary I got used to shallow friendships where we barely spoke about anything real. But Cindy was different. "Can I tell you something personal, like, about guys?" I asked.

"Of course," Cindy's eyes danced with excitement.

"Well, Jack told me that he couldn't stop thinking of me after I had given him the massage and he said that's rare for him. And then I told him about the situation in my life and how I wished that I had the money to just not worry about having to pay bills and all of that kind of thing. He said he could make it happen. He said he... he said that he wants one night with me and he'll make sure my dreams will come true."

I ventured a glance towards Cindy to gauge her reaction, but it was difficult to parse. I felt ashamed at even just saying it and I was sure that she was going to tell me I was stupid for letting this happen, but instead her face settled into a thoughtful expression.

"How much are we talking?" she asked.

"I don't know. He wasn't specific about that. I told him that I wasn't interested, but he gave me his card to call him. I just... I don't know if this is usual. I mean, I thought it was sweet that he rescued me and that he said he couldn't stop thinking about me, but then to come out with this... it's not normal, is it?"

"Not for people like you and me, but the rich live in a different world. He's used to buying and selling things all the time. It's probably some kind of kink for him. I bet he gets off on it. I mean... how do you feel about him?"

"Well, I find him attractive. I know that I should be appalled at the very thought of doing this. But money is money. I mean, I love my job, but it's never going to make me rich and now that I'm not with Mark I'm going to struggle to pay the bills. I've been struggling all my life and I just... I don't know how much more I can take. It's going to be the same struggle day in and day out and I just don't want any part of it." Emotions began to get the best of me again and came out in shuddering waves. A tear rolled down my cheek and landed in my cocoa with a splash. Thankfully it didn't ruin the taste.

"It might not always be that way," Cindy said, although her reassurance sounded hollow.

I stared into my cocoa as I opened up to her about Patrick and how he had humiliated me, and how I had gone from him straight to the arms of Mark who had abused me, and now I was left drifting in this directionless world without anything to point me in the right direction.

"You really haven't had the best luck with guys," Cindy said, looking at me with sympathy.

"No, I haven't. And I've never had anyone propose something like this either. I mean, should I just screw up his card, throw it away, and move on? I feel like I should be worth more than selling my body, but then I think about the money involved and it's only going to be one night, and it's not like I'm jeopardizing another love affair." The more I spoke the more I sounded as though I was trying to justify this decision. I didn't intend it to turn out that way, but I didn't want to simply dismiss it either.

"I'm not really the type of person to get caught up in sexual politics, but I do think this is a unique situation and I have to admit that if a handsome billionaire came into work and asked me for a happy ending, promising me a huge tip, well, I can't say that I wouldn't be tempted. I mean, it's your body and it's your choice. I guess one way to look at it is that it's just sex. I mean, you had it with Mark even though you didn't really love him, so is it that different to have sex with Jack? Maybe it's only a taboo because we've had it drilled into our heads from such a young age. It's not like you're going to do this regularly. It's a one time deal and with the money involved it might change your life. I guess it depends whether you can live with yourself afterwards. Can you be okay with it, or are you going to feel dirty? And I suppose you're going to have to think about the future as well. Would you be able to keep this from any potential romantic partners? A lot of people can be judgmental."

"I'm not sure I'd want to be with anyone who judges me for this. And I don't know if I'm going to be with anyone anyway. I don't think I was built for romance."

"I mean, there's no harm in calling him, is there? At least then you can see what it actually involves and how much he's paying. He might want to do some weird stuff and you don't want any part of that."

I nodded. The more I thought about it the more I wanted to call him. Maybe it was crazy of me, but I couldn't just pass this opportunity up. It might change my life, and there was something about Jack that played havoc with my mind as well. Perhaps it was just me trying to lash out at the world and be a little reckless after being controlled for so long as well. Life was meant to be lived and what kind of person was I going to be if I kept saying no to these things? I wasn't in a relationship so I wasn't betraying anyone, and I wasn't going to do anything sleazy. It was a simple transaction. Jack would benefit for one night, while I would take the money and use it to give myself a better life. As far as I could see there were no downsides, and since Cindy didn't seem strongly opposed to it either, I didn't feel as though I was crazy for thinking it.

We stayed up a little longer before I finally went to bed. I asked her if anything had happened with Blake, and she looked despondent. Apparently she got tired of dancing and went to the DJ booth to hang out with him for a little bit, hoping that he would take a break to dance with her, but he was dedicated to his job and as soon as he stopped working he was busy packing up his equipment. Cindy didn't seem too distressed; she was confident that there would be another chance. I wished her well. I was certain that I was never going to find love, but I hoped that she did. I knew it didn't touch everyone's life and it wasn't going to touch mine.

I wasn't like other people.

I never had been.

Chapter Thirteen

I gnawed on my lip as I sat in Cindy's kitchen, staring at the card Jack had given me. My body had been so tired it had surrendered to sleep and I felt well rested. Some parts of the previous night felt like a hazy dream. Even though I was holding Jack's card I couldn't quite believe that he had asked me to spend a night with him. Was my mind playing tricks on me? Mark had been calling me all night, leaving me voicemail messages where he begged me to take him back. He promised me the world, but it was too late for that. I knew he couldn't deliver on anything he promised and he wasn't going to convince me otherwise. It still took a lot of willpower for me to ignore them though. I was so used to running back to him and making amends, trying to fix the broken relationship. It had taken me a long time to realize that I was the only one interested in fixing it though. All he wanted to do was convince me that I was in the wrong.

I was more concerned with my future. I suppose that one good thing about having formed few emotional attachments was that I had developed a talent for being cold and cutting away my feelings when they were causing me harm. There had been a point where I used to get attached to friends at the orphanage, or foster parents who took me in for a short while, but these periods always ended. The people always disappeared from my life and it became too arduous to hold onto my feelings for them. It was less painful to just harden my heart and move on with my life, although I dreaded the idea of going back home to collect my things. I decided to leave that particular task for another day as I wanted to put some distance between myself and Mark. I worried that if I was in that place again and saw him I might break down. It would be better if I had something else going on in my life, or if I knew that I had financial security elsewhere.

And that's where Jack came in.

I dialed the number and felt my heart flutter as the phone rang. His deep mellifluous voice answered.

"Hey, Jack, it's Sandi," I said, wondering if he could hear the nervous tremors in my voice.

"Sandi, great, how are you doing? Are you feeling better after last night?"

"Yeah I am. I just... I wanted to discuss the proposal you made. I'm not ready to commit to it yet, but I would like to know more of what you have in mind."

He agreed and asked me out for a drink. I hadn't heard of the bar he suggested, but I assumed it was going to be something fancy considering his status in the world. Since I didn't have any of my own clothes with me I borrowed something of Cindy's; we were of a similar build, so while the dress wasn't a perfect fit it was good enough. It felt freeing to be able to wear something without getting involved in a massive argument about what was proper to wear. Going out had always been an exhausting endeavor because of Mark. Actually everything had been exhausting. Before I left Cindy wished me luck and reminded me that I didn't have to do anything I didn't want to do, even if the man was paying me millions.

*

I was right about the bar. It was called the Embassy Bar, located in an old building with grey pillars outside. It looked stately and official. I assumed that it was called the Embassy Bar because this place had once been an embassy. I felt self conscious as I looked at all these people who carried such confidence around with them. They looked as though they belonged here, with their elegant dresses, their tailored suits, and the gentle rhythm of intelligent conversation. It was a far cry from the bars that Mark and I had visited. They were always grimy, dirty things with stained glasses and dim lighting and the odor of years of neglect making the air stale. This place was light, as though I was walking into a hallowed place. The bar staff wore pristine outfits and greeted everyone with a smile. Delicate music tinkled in the background. Then I saw Jack, and my heart pitched. The man seemed to shimmer. I don't know how he managed it, but he looked larger than life. He wore a lazy smile. Not a hair was out of place on his head, and my attention was drawn directly to him.

A haze rose within my mind as he escorted me into a small corner of the bar. We sat at a circular table. Jack nodded towards strangers, who looked at me with curiosity and leaned in to share murmured whispers about this mystery companion of Jack's. I assumed they were asking themselves where I had appeared from and what someone like me was doing in a place like this. Jack signaled to a waiter and ordered a couple of drinks. I asked for a beer. Jack chuckled a little. I looked around and saw that all the other women were drinking wine from fluted glasses. There were unspoken rules here and it was as though I had stepped into another world. I suddenly felt as though I had made a huge mistake, but it was too late to retreat.

"I'm glad you called me. I'm also glad to see that you're looking better than you did last night," Jack said. I compared last night to this one. There we had been inside a cauldron of sweaty, dancing bodies. It was primal and savage, unlike this enlightened and elite place. There was no pounding music thundering through our hearts, and yet there was still an edge of excitement about what might happen.

"Yes, well, last night was interesting. Thank you again for what you did."

"Don't mention it. I'm just surprised that more people didn't come in to help."

"They did eventually I think. I believe many of them were shocked, and I think we're used to not getting involved in other people's business."

"I suppose so. Still. I'm glad you're safe. I worried about you last night when you left. I didn't like the idea of you going back to that maniac."

"I wasn't sure I liked the idea of it either, but it was something I had to do. Anyway, we had a conversation and it's... it's over. I told him that I didn't want to be with him anymore."

"And how did he take that?"

"Not very well. He's been calling me all day to try and talk with me, but I'm not going to give in. I know it's not healthy for me to stay in that relationship."

"That's something I'm inclined to toast to," he said, and raised his glass, clinking it against mine. I looked around and heard the murmured, hushed conversations occurring on the tables around us. Was Jack really prepared to talk about his proposed transaction in the midst of all these people? What might they do if they found out? "Jack, are you sure you want to speak about things here?" I cast a wary glance around.

Jack smirked. "Don't worry about anything. We're all discreet here and we'll be quiet. Have you had a chance to think about my offer?"

"I have and I'm still unsure about what exactly it entails."

"I thought that would have been obvious."

I flashed him a shy smile. "It is, I mean, I know the broad strokes, but I'm just wondering what exactly you expect from me. I mean," I leaned in and lowered my voice. "Are you into anything weird?"

A broad smile widened on Jack's face. "I know this kind of proposal isn't normal and I don't expect you to accept things without explanation, but I assure you that I wouldn't ask you to do anything you're uncomfortable with. It's simply that I am not a patient man and I do not have the time to pursue a romantic relationship with all the tangle of emotions that one requires. My life is devoted to work, so I don't have room in my schedule for things like dates. So I am willing to pay to... accelerate matters and enjoy an intimate night. There is nothing tawdry or clandestine about it. It's simply a matter of having the money to let things develop on my own terms. I want to spend the night with you, and I'm willing to pay you generously."

Jack was so blunt with his words in a way that thrilled me. He had the kind of confidence that I always admired, probably because it was absent within my heart. He was the kind of person I wished I could be.

"And how much are we talking?" I asked, taking a mouthful of beer.

Jack pursed his lips and stared at me intently. The worth of things was almost a foreign concept to him because he could afford anything he wanted, but what price was a human life? What price was my dignity?

"One hundred," he said.

I frowned and almost spat out my beer. "A hundred? Jack you have to be kidding me. I knew there was going to be some catch." For such rich people billionaires had to be the cheapest ones in the world, I suppose they had to be in order to hoard their wealth. I was about ready to rise from the table, unable to believe that he would reward my time like this. He must have thought I had no self respect at all if he thought I was willing to sell myself for one night for a hundred bucks. I was angry at myself for ever thinking this was a possibility in the first place. But before I could rise in anger Jack spoke again.

"One hundred thousand," he clarified.

"Oh," I said, suddenly struck dumb. It was pocket change for him, but for me it was a life changing amount. It was hard to imagine what I might do with all that money. I wouldn't have to struggle every month. I could invest in things and get a better place to live. I would actually be able to interact with the world in a meaningful way, feeling like I could contribute. But then I wondered if I should push for more. While I was thinking about this he continued speaking.

"You said that you wanted an amount that would change your life, and I think that counts. It's just for one night as well, rather than an ongoing thing. And if you like I could put you in touch with a financial advisor to help you manage your money. People who suddenly come into a lot of cash often find themselves frittering it away easily because they don't know how to manage it."

A hundred thousand dollars for one night, and it wasn't as though I even had to force myself to be attracted to this man. I had been involved with men who hurt me before, who had left me feeling empty and desolate. I thought perhaps it was time that I turned the tables. It was time for me to get something out of life. Cindy had said I should think about whether I could live with myself for spending a night with Jack. I knew that I could. In fact I felt stupid for even considering walking away from the opportunity.

I gradually agreed, not wanting to seem too desperate. We spoke about the particulars of the matter to ensure that we were both safe and understood what we expected from each other. He made sure to tell me that this was not going to lead to a relationship because he wasn't interested in something like that, and I made it clear that just because he was paying for a night with me that didn't mean I was going to do anything he wanted. Eventually we had everything agreed and we finished our drinks.

"Shall we go now?" he asked.

I didn't realize he meant this night. Suddenly nerves fluttered inside and I started to think about reasons to turn away. I needed more time to think about it, more time to process what I was doing. But then again having a hundred grand was just about enough to curb my nerves. I nodded silently, telling myself that I just had to keep calm and that everything was going to be okay. It was strange, but as we left the bar I found myself hoping that I was worth a hundred grand. After all, I had only been with one guy and Mark had never been proactive with his praise. I hoped that Jack wouldn't end up feeling like he wasted his money.

Chapter Fourteen

We were in his apartment again. The air was seared with tension between us. We both knew what was coming, and yet I was still nervous. He made me a drink and transferred a portion of the money over to my bank account straight away, as a sign of goodwill. Then he came to the couch and pushed away a strand of hair from my face.

"You really are beautiful," he said. The gaze in his eyes was intense and I almost couldn't bear it. My skin felt as though it was on fire. Suddenly I was aware of his hand resting on my thigh, as though it had always been there. I told myself that I shouldn't be ashamed, that I shouldn't doubt myself. Nobody else ever had to know, and who were they to judge anyway? I had a chance to make a hundred grand and I would have been stupid not to take it, especially when Jack was so handsome, with his chiseled jaw and piercing eyes. All I had to do was let myself drown in my natural attraction to him and try to forget about the money that was on the line.

He leaned in and all of a sudden the air was awash with his warm breath. His lips brushed my cheek before they drifted down and plucked a kiss from my lips. My eyelids closed and a soft moan burst out, although it was quickly suffocated by his ardent kiss. His lips were firm but tender, his kiss imbued with passion. His hand curled around the back of my neck as my body melted underneath him, feeling the strength and the weight of him overwhelm me. It felt as though he had been holding something deep inside him for so long and now it was free again. My hands drifted down the hard angles of his body, pawing at his shirt, feeling the scorching warmth of his flesh underneath. I was caught in a world that was vivid with desire, and it was all driven by him. Our tongues danced and I allowed myself to ride the natural feelings that rose within me. I embraced him and kissed him back. It was surprisingly wonderful to be lost in throes with someone without the fear of them hitting or choking me, or feeling like they were making love to me as a punishment.

Jack moved away from my mouth and left a trail of tingling kisses down my neck, his warm breath making me shudder as it washed over my skin. I arched my head back, offering him the hollow of my throat. His lips trailed down the soft beads of sweat that formed on my skin. His hands rested around my waist, powerful and strong. Descending down my body, he stopped as he was on his knees and then looked up at me. I'll never forget the look in his eyes. I could tell that something deep inside him was being unleashed. I had felt the tension inside his body when I massaged him. At the time I assumed it was a result of his stressful lifestyle, but now I realized that a lot of it was pent up sexual energy as well, and I was going to be the one who bore the brunt of it all.

He rose from his knees, towering over me. Jack offered me his hand. I took it without hesitation. He clasped my hand and then led me away. My heart thundered and a knot of tension twitched. I wasn't sure what awaited me, but I was excited, and not just because it was going to be a huge payday.

His bed was wide and long. Scarlet silk sheets were draped over the firm mattress. The curtains were drawn and moonlight poured in, framing the bed in a spotlight. He took me in his arms again, kissing me hard and deep. He was tall and strong enough to lift me onto my tiptoes. My hair flowed through his fingers. His kiss seemed to reach deep inside me, as though he was touching my very soul. I felt as though something was opening up and blossoming within me, as though he was peeling away the outer layer and getting to everything that I held within, everything that I hid from the world. I pressed my body against his and draped my arms around his neck, clinging onto him as though I was drowning and he was my only hope of salvation. Our kisses were deep and I could feel the tension rippling all over the expanse of his body. The air crackled as his hands drifted down my body, resting on my waist. I rolled back on my heels, feeling as though the world lurched around me. He placed a finger under my chin and tilted my head up, gazing deep into my eyes. I wanted to ask him what he saw and what he felt, but I was too scared. There was an intensity about the moment that I couldn't quite shake, and it struck a chord within my heart.

We kissed again as we fell to the bed. His hands were everywhere, sliding over my breasts and stomach, running down my legs, as though there was no place that was free from his influence. I ran my hands through his mane of hair, so thick and lustrous. His lips were smooth, and his muscles burned with vibrant energy. I groaned as we rose to our knees, kneeling opposite each other. I gazed at the broad expanse of his chest. It was as though all the essence of masculinity had been poured into him and now he bristled with this intoxicating, intense energy that proved to be irresistible. He pushed away the straps of my dress. It was such a casual stroke of his hands, and yet it meant so much. My shoulders were exposed and the dress hung down, threatening to reveal my plunging cleavage. I could sense the hunger in him, as though he was a wolf and I was mere prey that he was waiting to claim. He kissed me lightly again as he reached around and unzipped my dress. I felt the silky fabric brushing against my skin as he pulled it away. He drew back as I shrugged off the dress and tossed it aside. His hands rested against the curve of my waist and then rose, tugging at my bra straps. I deftly unbuttoned his shirt and opened it up to reveal his torso. The muscles were taut and it was covered in dark hair. A low growl emanated from my throat. My gaze was transfixed upon him. I pushed the shirt away. It wasn't the first time I had seen him like this, but there was a different energy to things now.

We caressed each other, tracing our fingers over our aching flesh. I fumbled with his belt, unclasping the leather and pulling it away. I was more confident than I usually would have been, buoyed by the fact that he was paying me so much money. He wasn't with me out of pity or sympathy. He wanted me, and he was willing to put his money where it counted.

His thick fingers were surprisingly deft as they slipped my bra away easily, freeing my breasts. They poured out and his hands immediately came around to caress the soft skin and tease the hard nipples. He traced a line down the rising curves and kissed down the middle of my chest. My body arched back, supported by his trunk of an arm, as he kissed and teased me. As his teeth nibbled gently waves of ecstatic pleasure swarmed my body and I trembled. His free hand ran down the middle of my body and squeezed my thigh; his roaming fingers threatened to brush against my femininity but they always seemed just an inch away, achingly so. I began to whimper as heat rose within me. I could feel his hard arousal pressing against me. I fumbled myself away from him so that I could touch him and look at the bulge. I stripped him of his clothes and saw him again, this time taking in his manhood properly. When I had seen it before I had been shocked by the abrupt reveal of him, and had been embarrassed at the impropriety of the moment, but now there was no such hesitation within me. I could admire the impressive stature of him. Like the rest of him it was giant and thick, with wide veins rippling around the long shaft. The tip was smooth, and a thatch of neatly trimmed hair rested around the base. As I reached out towards him I could feel the radiating heat emanating from him. My fingers curled around the shaft and his head arched back. His eyes closed, and a long, low murmur escaped his lips. I stroked him gently and slowly, gradually becoming more aware of what he liked, and adjusting the movements of my wrist accordingly.

My gaze swam along the sea of his flesh as I gently pushed him down until he was flat on his back. I twisted my hand, enjoying the sight of a smile flickering on his face. I could feel the tension rising with him and spread my other hand out over his stomach so that I could touch the tremors of his body and be aware of the twisting storm I was creating within him. I knew what he wanted; he had asked for it after I had given him a massage. Maybe Mark was right; maybe being a masseuse was just one step away from being a whore, but when it came to Jack I didn't particularly care. The man was gorgeous and every inch of him was alluring. It might well have been the professional streak in me as well, but I was determined to earn every cent of the small fortune he promised me.

I lowered my head and breathed in the masculine musk that rose in a haze from his manhood. My hand slipped down to the base of his shaft and I brought it to rest against my cheek, feeling a stream of heat smear towards my mouth. My hair draped down and touched his thighs as I opened my lips and took him into the warm, willing cavern where my tongue slid around him. I closed my eyes. His grunts were music to my ears. My tongue was a tornado and when I brought my head back to allow my aching jaws a brief respite I brought a thread of saliva with me. His erection glistened in the silver light that illuminated us, and I dove down again for another taste, feeling the heat of him resting against my tongue. My head bobbed up and down as I took every inch of him inside me, feeling the sweet ache in the back of my throat as I struggled with his length. Jack gasped and groaned. His hands rested around my scalp as I brought him closer and closer to that sweet climax. I breathed deeply and ignored my aching jaws before he pulled my head away and flipped me onto my back.

Breath was driven from my lungs as I groaned.

"I have a lot in me and I'm not ready to give it to you yet," he growled, moving so that his shadow covered my entire body. As he kissed me his hand moved down and tugged at the hem of my panties, slowly peeling away the dark lace that covered my most intimate area. Instinctively I squirmed, but I was ready to give him everything. He murmured in my ear and as he pressed his palm flat against me we could both feel the damp arousal that was already gathering in between my thighs. I groaned as he teased me, drifting light touches up and down my burning thigh, before he finally delved into me.

It felt as though a bolt of lightning shot through me, and yet at the same time it all originated in my molten core. One finger slipped inside me and it made the world twist and turn. Excited beads of sweat trickled down my naked skin, and heat flushed through me, as though I had succumbed to a fever. The flashing delight made my head twist and turn. His finger curled within me, beckoning forth the power and the glory, my body was seized with some almighty delight that crackled like fire and rampaged through me like an earthquake. I had to turn my head away from his kisses as I gasped for breath. He continued, trailing his lips down past my collarbone and onto my breasts. I groaned and murmured. It had never been this way with Mark. I had never been able to surrender this fully. As he slid over me I pressed my hand against the sinews of his back, feeling the writhing energy that surged within him. I felt as though I was throbbing all over, as though I was ready to explode. I didn't understand how he could do so much with just one finger, and yet I was not going to complain or decry this miracle. My body felt like a puppet and he was the one holding the strings.

I could taste salty sweet sweat upon my lips as I gasped for breath. Hair was in my face, falling over my eyes like a veil, and next to me was him in all his glory. He seemed to glow in this sizzling way, as though he wasn't really a man at all but some god venturing down to toy and tease with a mortal. Everything that was within me unspooled, as though he was undoing all the tension that had built up over the years, just as I had done when I had massaged him; the difference was that he was massaging me from the inside.

I groaned and cupped his head as he continued to move his finger inside me. I wanted him more than anything in that moment. I didn't care about the money or that I was some forgotten orphan who didn't have anything to my name. When I looked into his eyes I felt as though he was truly seeing me, as though I mattered, and I clung to him desperately. Passionate pleasure rose in a huge crescendo and then crashed through me in one long tidal wave, churning up my insides. I felt it all over me, in my curling toes and my trembling fingers. I melted inside, my head lolling with my lips parted, and still Jack continued. It was as though he didn't know when to stop, and I wasn't sure that I wanted him to.

Relentless pleasure crashed through me again and again and again without mercy. There was nothing I could do but surrender to it, letting it wash over me in foamy waves that were oh so glorious and tempting. Golden fire gleamed within me, as though Jack had unlocked something deep and wonderful, some hidden treasure that nobody else had been able to find. I could feel everything pouring out of me in a blissful stream. It stained my thighs and when he drew his hands away they were sticky sweet. He stroked my cheek and I could breath in my own sweet scent. I kissed his palm and brushed my lips against his fingers, getting a taste of me. Then he kissed me, and we were lost in a heavenly world of lust.

Jack shifted his body over me. His weight was crushing and comfortable. Our limbs entwined together, the two bodies becoming one. I tilted my neck and watched him through blurred, bleary vision, gazing in awe at the sight of his impressive manhood pressing against me and then gasping at the feeling of him sliding inside me. Pain blurred with pleasure and in all honesty I wasn't sure what I should be feeling. All I knew is that it left me reeling.

For a moment we stayed like that, enjoying the feeling of our bodies melting into each other. Our skin sizzled with sweat and it felt as though we were becoming one. I found it impossible to tell where he ended and I began. Then he kissed me, and then he thrust. With every movement it felt as though the world rocked. Quaking sensations crashed through me and around me. My mind was alive with these crazy feelings and I wasn't sure how I should process them. It was all a chaotic blur, wild and intense, and all I could do was lay back and let them seize me. His strong body thrust over and over again, and mine responded with the same rhythm. My lithe curves were dominated by his bristling muscles. All the masculine heat scorched me, but I welcomed the pain. I clung onto him as though if I let go I would fall into oblivion. With every moment he released another part of himself within me, gradually getting more ardent and more frenzied until it felt as though my body was going to snap in two under the intense strength of his passion. His fingers dug into my flesh and I dragged my nails down his back, screaming as I braced myself against the ruthless sensations. He pressed his forehead against mine and then buried his head next to my neck. The flurry of sweat and breath flashed and then my body arched as he crashed into me, getting deeper and deeper until there was nothing left to explore, until there was no part of me that hadn't been touched by him.

Jack's body rumbled like a churning volcano. I could feel the violent fury growing within him and I was almost scared to embrace the final explosion. It felt as though I was at the top of the rollercoaster. All there was left to do was plummet at impossible speeds, but a part of me wanted to remain frozen, suspended in that sweet moment of anticipation. But Jack had other intentions. He was like a juggernaut. Something was happening in him that couldn't be stopped. His body was a blur as he made love to me, releasing all the tension in one huge tempestuous burst that soared through me in a burst of fire.

The world raged around me, a cacophony of passion and heat. For a moment it felt as if everything had been set ablaze by our lust, but then it faded. Sweat tinged our skin. Our chests rose and heaved with deep breaths. I was drained and delirious. It felt as though I had touched heaven, and I wasn't sure my body would ever be the same again.

"Looks like I got my happy ending in the end," he growled, his words punctuated by deep gasps. I smiled as I lay back against the pillow, my head still swimming with everything I had just experienced. I swallowed deeply and closed my eyes, not feeling one iota of regret.

Chapter Fifteen

The morning sun broke through the window in golden strands. My body ached from our vigorous night together. We had made love for hours well into the depth of the night, before sleep had eventually overcome us. I was certain that Jack had gotten his money's worth. Delight still played in my mind. Jack was sleeping soundly, breathing in deeply, his face peaceful after he had released so much of his tension. Making love with him was far different than with Mark. Mark had always been concerned only with his own pleasure, and only shared it with me when he felt like it. I was just an instrument for his amusement. If he wanted to be aggressive then he would be aggressive. If he wanted to be quick then he would be quick. My needs never mattered to him, and while I wasn't sure that they mattered to Jack, he at least had made it feel like we were making love together rather than it being something he was doing to me.

Not that I was letting myself get carried away. I knew the terms of the agreement. This was a one night affair with no strings attached at all. We had spoken at length about the nuances of what was going to happen. I was on the pill so there was no fear about an unexpected pregnancy, and I wasn't looking to fall in love anyway. After my relationship with Mark I think I needed to really examine myself and what I wanted in life. After all, I was only in my twenties. I still had a lot of life left to live and a lot of opportunities to experience all that I had missed out on.

It was strange to see him like this. In the massage parlor everything had had a different context. He had been a client then, no different than anyone else who wandered in off the street. But I had known from the first moment that there was something different about him. There had been an attraction there, and now I had experienced what it was like to make love to a billionaire. Even in the light of a new day I didn't regret what I had done. I had a cherished memory of a night with a wonderful man to keep the embers burning, and I had made a hundred grand, which was enough to give me a new start.

I rose and had a shower, before getting dressed again. When I walked into the lounge Jack was awake, cooking breakfast. He offered me some, and I accepted. He wore loose pajama pants and didn't seem interested in covering up his torso, and I certainly wasn't complaining. For a moment I was afraid that there would be some awkwardness, but I suppose I shouldn't have been worried. He was a businessman after all.

"I just transferred the rest of your money into your account. Thank you for a wonderful night. It was exactly what I needed," he said.

"I'm glad I could help. To be honest I think I needed it as well. My experiences with men haven't all been good."

"Well, hopefully this is a chance for you to make a new change in your life. Do you know what you're going to do with the money?"

"I'm going to get a better place first I think, and then I'll probably look to travel. I need to rediscover myself and find out what I really want in life. I've let myself be defined by other factors too often," I admitted. Jack nodded. "Is there anywhere that you would recommend?"

"I'm afraid I can't help you with that. I have been to a few different countries, but they were for business trips so I haven't been to places as a tourist. I'm sure there are plenty of other resources for you to look at though," he said. I glanced around at the ornaments on display and was a little surprised that he hadn't been traveling.

"Oh, I just assumed that you had spent some time traveling given the things you have on display here."

"I picked them up at auctions. I just found them interesting. I did intend to go traveling when I was younger, but then Dad gave me some extra responsibility with the company so I found that I couldn't leave. But I'm sure you'll have a lot of fun."

I arched my eyebrows in surprise. It still amazed me that Jack had all the opportunity in the world to leave and yet he stayed in the same place, rooted to his duty and his obligations.

"Haven't you ever been tempted to delegate some of your responsibility to someone else so that you can experience a few things the world has to offer?" I asked.

Jack smirked as he served up a plate of eggs and bacon. "I have, but it's never quite worked out in the end. I suppose I'm too much like my father in that regard. I just can't quite let things go. Whenever anyone else takes over I see what they're doing wrong and I have to correct them. And if I left I'd just be worried that they were making suboptimal decisions that the company will suffer from. It's too risky, so here is where I stay."

I thought about how I had been trapped by the circumstances of my life and it struck me that there were some similarities between me and Jack. He had been born into this dynasty, forced to take his place as the leader of a company even though he might have preferred to do other things.

"Do you ever wish you had been born to different parents? Do you ever wish you had another life, one where you could have pursued different interests and had the chance to experience the world?"

Jack tilted his head and then shrugged. "This is the only life for me. This is what I was born to do." He spoke with such certainty that I envied him. it must have been nice to be confident about his place in the world and his role within it. I was yet to find my niche.

"But aren't you worried that your life is going to get stale? With you having such a regimented routine isn't there a risk that it's going to get boring? Where's the excitement?"

"Excitement is overrated," Jack said, and didn't offer any elaboration on his point. He was a most intriguing man, and not at all what I had expected from a billionaire. I had to assume there were things he was not telling me about his life because he was a private man and I had only touched his soul briefly, but there was something about him that was entirely compelling. He had a way of thinking that was so far removed from my own mind that I wanted to delve deeper and understand him. Of course I wasn't going to be given the chance because our night was at an end, and one night with him was all I was going to be given.

We shared breakfast and I had to start to think about the rest of my life. My eyes boggled when I looked at my bank balance and saw the large amount. The world was open to me in a way that it had never been before. I finally had means by which I could take my destiny into my own hands. I felt more confident than I had before, although I wasn't sure how much of that was due to the money and how much was due to the effect that Jack had on me. We spoke for a little while longer until our plates were clean, and then it was time for me to leave. He shook my hand and our gaze met for one final time. I felt the thrill of attraction again, and wondered if he shared the same. But I didn't ask him about it. He had made it firmly clear that he wasn't interested in a relationship. His life was a strict routine and he didn't have room for me, so I shouldn't waste time thinking about him.

But as my hand slipped away from his and I turned to leave his apartment there was a part of me that wondered what it might be like to share a life with him, to show him that perhaps excitement wasn't as overrated as he thought. There was something alluring about the challenge of being the woman who was able to wrest him from his work, but all I could do was sigh and chastise myself for entertaining a silly little daydream. I descended the elevator and left Jack behind, ready to embrace this new phase of my life, excited to see what would happen next.

Chapter Sixteen

Sandi left me in silence. Silence was one of the few constants in my life. It's always there around me, accompanying me, always ready to slither in beside me after I've had others in my company. I walked to my window and gazed down at the street below, trying to pick her out of the crowd, but it was impossible from this height. Everyone looks the same. I glanced around at the ornaments I had collected, feeling oddly ashamed that I had bought them at auction rather than having found them myself in the far reaches of the world. The look on Sandi's face hadn't escaped me. I knew she believed that I had wasted my wealth and the opportunities given to me, but what else could I do? The company needed me. I couldn't very well abandon it to someone who didn't know what they were doing. Perhaps in a way I was trapped by my legacy, but it was the only purpose I had. What use was being frivolous with my money? Being rich wasn't an excuse to be lax with my wealth; it meant that I had to be more responsible.

But still... I did wonder what my life would have been like if I had had different parents. Would I have had the same work ethic? Would I have lived such a lonely life?

I walked back into my bedroom and sat on the bed, placing my hand on the soft sheets. They were still warm. I leaned down and inhaled deeply. Sandi's sweet scent still lingered in the air. I closed my eyes and let myself swim in the memories of tasting her supple flesh and feeling her body yield under my strength. Her kisses were sweet and tantalizing. Her femininity was alluring. Every kiss was delicious and she managed to elicit a fierce desire from me. The pleasure had flowed through me in a way that I had not anticipated. There was something about her that made me feel intoxicated and out of control. I had been filled with a wild abandon that spoke to the most savage and most instinctual part of my soul. With her I was an animal, letting my civility slough away, and I had drank deeply from the lack of her seductive aura.

It was rare for anyone to have this commanding effect over me, especially a woman. It was a great source of pride for me that I had never let myself become weak in the presence of the fairer sex. I had seen too many of my peers being brought down by sex scandals and affairs because they had let their instincts ruin them. I was not the same as them. I was not going to be a slave to my desires. And yet with Sandi that had happened. I had been filled with an uncontrollable urge to drown into her body. I was drawn to her inexorably, as though my body was completely in control and I had no sense of restraint at all.

I had been a wild stallion through the night. I thought it would have been enough to get it out of my system, but instead it had given life to a new hunger. I had been tempted to ask Sandi to stay, but had bit my tongue at the last moment. We had agreed to certain terms and it would be rude of me to suggest an alteration to the agreement now. Besides, I couldn't keep funneling money to her. One night was an odd occurrence, but a frequent payment was something else entirely. The more often it happened the more likely it was that the truth was going to get out, and I wasn't prepared for the hit to my reputation that it would take. Besides, I hadn't lied to her. My life did not have room for a relationship, and that was not going to change. She seemed excited about exploring the world and that was her prerogative. I had seen all I needed to see. I wished her the best of luck, and hoped that she would find a man who was not so quick with his fists.

*

Days turned into weeks. I fell back into my regular routine and while it was comforting I was unsettled by the fact that I couldn't stop thinking about Sandi. It was most unusual. Occasionally a thought would drift into my mind when I least expected it and I was flushed with desire again. I was filled with a thought of delving into her curves and breathing in her womanly scent, of my hands sinking into her supple skin and feeling her respond with yearning moans. They came at the most inopportune times and I wasn't sure what was wrong with me because I had never been so taken with a woman before. I did think about stopping by the massage parlor to see her again, but I knew it would only lead to trouble. I threw myself into my work, expecting that this was just a symptom of our night together and that these sensations would fade soon enough, but they still persisted and I wasn't prepared for this.

One hundred thousand dollars had seemed an adequate price for a night of passion, and it was a substantial enough sum that it would afford Sandi the ability to pursue a new life in whatever avenue she wished, escaping the trauma that her ex boyfriend had placed upon her. I had paid her for one night, and one night was all I expected to get from her, so the fact that she remained in my mind was very surprising. It was supposed to have been nothing more than a physical release, something to take the edge off my tension and allow me to indulge in something that was so intrinsic to humanity. But I hadn't been prepared for the lingering emotional effects and I felt stupid for being so weak. I was supposed to be strong, and I wouldn't let myself fall into the trap of being enraptured by a woman. It wasn't time for that yet. I still had too much work to do when it came to my company.

*

I was sitting in my office quelling thoughts of Sandi from my mind, focusing on various accounts and paperwork that had found their way to me. Work had always been a refuge for me. It had worked when Mom died, and I was certain that it would help me through this too. The longer Sandi remained on my mind the harder it became to push her from it, and the more I worried that she would remain there for years. I steeled myself against my feelings and tried to bury them deep down inside me, even though I had a feeling it would be futile. Then I received a call that changed my life. It was my father's carer, telling me that he had died.

I listened to the words but couldn't quite believe them. I leaned back in my chair, glad that I was sitting down because otherwise I would have fallen to the floor in shock. I didn't want to believe it. I couldn't believe it, but I had to. Dad had always taught me to compartmentalize my emotions so that they wouldn't interfere with my business acumen. As a result I had developed a hard heart and it was always difficult for emotions to penetrate them. Even now, upon hearing of his death, it felt like a stone of sorrow replaced my heart. I felt numb and cold, as though the world was closing in on me and a shadow fell across the sky. I felt removed from my body, as though I was just a shell. I listened to the words, but I could not react.

She told me that Dad had been complaining of chest pains, but they didn't think anything of it. Then she had gone to wake him in the morning and found him dead. A life could be gone in the blink of an eye, plucked from the world as easily as a flower would be plucked from a meadow. It seemed wrong somehow that Dad should have gone so quietly. He was always a man of thunder, storming through the world demanding rather than asking, and everyone acquiesced to him because they knew they had no other choice. When I was a child I believed he could do anything. He was larger than life, like a god made of flesh and blood. But as the years had gone by there were chinks in his perceived omnipotence. He hadn't been able to stop the ravages of aging, nor had he been able to prevent illness from taking Mom from us. But that had been easier to cope with. Mom had been ill for a long time and when she died it was more of a relief than anything else. At least she had been put out of her misery and was at peace. Dad still had a lot to offer. Sure he was old, but his mind was sharp and his energy was not diminished. I felt guilty for practically putting him on bed rest and not spending as much time with him as I should have. I had dismissed his desire to return to work and pushed him away because he was retired, and now he was gone. I would never see him again, and now I was the last of my family left. The burden weighed heavily on my shoulders. I thanked the carer for letting me know, and then rubbed my temples. As a matter of course I called in my assistant and told her to arrange a funeral for my father, all the while I felt cold grief spread its icy fingers within me. I hadn't been prepared for this, not to be all alone. Dad still had a good few years left in him. He still had time, and it only made me wonder how much time I had left.

Was I really stoic enough to spend the rest of my life alone?

Chapter Seventeen

Weeks had passed and to be honest my life hadn't changed as much as I thought it would. For the moment I was still working in the massage parlor because I didn't know what else to do with my time. I was trying to figure out the best plan, and I was still living with Cindy because I liked the company and I thought buying a place was pointless if I was going traveling. I just had to decide where. I had decided not to tell Ally how I had received this money, and lied that I had won the lottery. Cindy aided me in telling this lie because it was easier than telling people that I had spent the night with a billionaire.

And what a night it had been.

I had tried to forget about the time we spent together for my own sake. It didn't do me any good to think about what might have been. Jack was living his own life and I had to do the same, but I was damned if his lazy smile and brooding eyes didn't haunt my dreams. A nightly fire was stoked in my body as I drifted back to that night when pleasure blazed within me. Flashes of passion burst within me as I remembered his fingers curling inside me and his lips leaving blazing kisses all over my skin. It was as though something had been awakened inside me during that night, and I couldn't let it go.

Perhaps there was some part of me that just wanted to torture myself. That was the only explanation I could give for the way I was feeling. There was no reason to let myself be tied to Jack in any way, and yet it felt as though there was some thread connecting us even though we had both gone our separate ways. Even if there was a chance of seeing him again I knew it was pointless because we lived in different worlds. If he was ever going to end up with anyone it should have been with someone who could be a princess, not a lowly orphan like me.

I tried to focus on the positives and the fact that I had a hundred thousand dollars in the bank, and a whole lot of possibilities. I did a bit of reading about how to handle money and I was surprised to find that most people who came into a fortune suddenly, blew it all quickly because they had no idea how to manage such a vast sum. I vowed to myself that I wasn't going to be like them. Jack had given me the details of a financial manager so I decided to go and see him. There was enough money that I figured I could invest some in stocks or whatever, and use the rest to treat myself. I was still working at the massage parlor for the time being because I liked the company and, frankly, I wanted something to fill my time. There was also a niggling whisper in the back of my mind that told me Jack might come in. It was stupid, but every time the door opened I looked up in the vain hope that he would be standing there, and every time my heart was filled with inevitable disappointment. I tried to not torture myself, and I knew that the sooner I got out of the country the better. I could reset my life and figure out what I wanted to do with the rest of my time on earth. I had been given this gift, and I wasn't going to squander it.

But I had to return to the past and get my things. I couldn't borrow Cindy's clothes forever, and there were a few items I missed. My throat clenched when I sent Mark a message to tell him when I was intending to come over, and that to make things easier he shouldn't be there. I picked a time when he was likely to be working to increase the chances of him being absent. Cindy insisted that she come with me, just in case. The company would be welcome, and the two of us working would make the task pass all the more quickly, so I agreed.

Mark's messages and calls decreased, although they were still present. I had learned to ignore my phone because it was almost always him either being angry or repentant. It amazed me that he couldn't see how unbalanced he was, and now that I had gained some distance from the relationship I was angry at myself for not seeing it sooner. Being with Mark had clouded my judgment, and I was just glad that I had managed to escape the abyss before it completely swallowed me up.

*

The day that we went back to the house to pick up my things was a sunny day. Light was shed on the decrepit neighborhood. It was a sobering sight. I wasn't sorry to leave it. I walked up to the house and turned the key in the lock, only to find that it was open. I groaned inwardly as I pushed the door open and saw Mark standing in the lounge. He had been pacing, and when he saw me enter his gaze flashed towards me and he rushed from the lounge to the door, only hesitating when he saw that Cindy accompanied me. I rolled my eyes and my heart sank. This should have been an easy task, but I should have expected Mark to make it more complicated than it needed to be.

"Mark, what are you doing here? I asked you to be somewhere else while I pack up my stuff," I said, unable to prevent the aggrieved tone from making my voice sound shrill.

"I know you did, but I couldn't Sandi. You haven't been replying to my texts or answering my calls. All I want is to speak with you. It's been hell without you Sandi. I haven't been able to sleep. I haven't been able to think straight. It's all been a mess without you and I don't know what to do. I don't know how I can go on like this," he pleaded. His skin was paler than usual and there were shadows under his eyes. He wore a baggy football jersey, which swayed and sagged as he gestured with his arms.

"That's not my problem," I said firmly. I had told myself that I wasn't going to give him any reason to suspect there was a chance for us to get back together.

"Sandi, come on, I know I haven't been the best boyfriend in the past but I can learn. I can change. I love you, you know that I have from the first moment we met. Don't you remember? Back then you didn't even want company but I could tell there was something between us. I stayed by your side and bought you drink after drink and eventually you opened up to me. You liked that I was persistent. I swore to myself that night that I wasn't going to leave without getting your number, and I'm going to be persistent now. I don't want things to end between us Sandi. We're supposed to be together forever, no matter what. I can change. I can make things right. I promise I won't do anything like that to you again. I'll be good. I'll go to counseling. I'll do whatever it takes for this to work again."

I had never seen him look so damned desperate before. He was vulnerable, like a child afraid of losing their parents. It was then that I realized I had had the power in the relationship this whole time. I almost laughed because I had always been the one who had been afraid, when it was Mark who had been scared. He was the one afraid of losing me, so he had held on so tightly, squeezing so hard that I had slipped through his fingers. He'd built up his world in such a way that he couldn't imagine himself existing without me, but that was his fantasy, not my reality.

Cindy glanced towards me, standing ready to aid me if I needed it. I appreciated her support and I hoped she knew what a good friend she was being when I needed one most.

"I'm glad that you're willing to take steps to address the problem Mark, but it's too late for that. If you had said this a year ago then maybe things would be different, but I've changed and I've realized that I can't be my best self with you. I want you to get better and get healthy, but it's not going to be with me. I can't give anymore of myself to this relationship," I said. I could see the emotions rippling over his face. Despite what he said he was the same old Mark, and I knew the fury was bristling under the surface.

"That's not fair Sandi. Come on, after all I've done for you, you owe me this chance."

"That's the problem though Mark, this isn't your first chance. I've given you chance after chance before and nothing has changed. If I come back now then you're never going to understand that there are consequences for your actions. You can't treat me like this and expect me to keep coming back. This is the end, and you need to accept that."

"I can't," he said. Tears filled his eyes and his hands curled into tight balls. His cheeks became flushed with anger.

"You have to."

"I won't. I'm devoted to you Sandi. What does this stuff matter compared to all the years we're going to spend together? When we're old and grey and we look back on our lives this stuff isn't going to matter. I'm going to keep chasing you and keep reminding you that I love you. I'm not going to give up on you Sandi. I'll do whatever it takes to prove that we're meant to be together."

I knew that he meant it, and the thought of him stalking me through eternity made me shudder.

"If you do that she'll just get a restraining order," Cindy said, but that didn't deter Mark.

"I don't care. I'll go to jail for you Sandi. I'll do whatever it takes to show you that I'm serious."

"It doesn't matter Mark because I'm not going to be in the country. I'm going traveling and even I don't know where I'm going yet so there's no way that you can follow me. I'm going to have an adventure and get away from this place, and there's nothing anyone can do to stop me. And you can wait for me if you want, but there's no guarantee that I'm ever going to come back. You can say all this and you can do all this, but it's not going to change my mind. I don't want to be with you. I'm not going to be a prisoner of your emotions any longer."

Mark's face twisted as he processed what I was saying. I could see the uncertainty and the disbelief flicker across his features, before he eventually scowled in derision and shook his head.

"There's no way you're leaving. You don't have it in you. Besides, how the hell are you going to afford it? I know you haven't saved up enough money from your job. Or have you started to give out little bonuses to your clients? Have you finally turned into something I was always afraid of?"

Cindy started forward, aghast at what Mark was saying. "You have no right to say that! If you must know Sandi won-" I raised a hand to interrupt her before she finished. Sure, I could have told Mark the same lie I had told Ally to prevent anyone from judging me harshly, but I knew that I had to take ownership of my decisions. I wanted Mark to know the truth, to really understand the person I had become and what he had driven me to do. I wasn't ashamed of what I had done, so there was no need to hide behind it. Besides, I knew it would drive him crazy as well.

"Actually Mark the man who saved me after you tried to drag me home was a billionaire. And actually he came into the massage parlor and asked me for a happy ending, but I told him no because I was loyal to you. Then he told me that he couldn't stop thinking about me and that he would pay me a hundred thousand dollars to spend the night with him, so I did. I knew I didn't have a future with you so there was no point in denying the opportunity to set myself up for life. I sacrificed one night so that I could have the chance to escape this place and escape you. Those are the lengths I'm willing to go to," I lowered my voice on those last few words, hoping that he'd realize how serious I was.

"You whore," he said in a low rasp. White hot rage glowed in his eyes. He clenched his fists so tightly that I almost expected blood to pour from his palms. I backed away, afraid that I had made a miscalculation and that it had only enraged him to a point where he would punish me for these crimes I had committed. Mark stormed towards me. Cindy and I both cowered, but he pushed past us and walked out of the house, muttering dark things to himself.

Cindy and I breathed a sigh of relief as we glanced at each other.

"That was close. I really thought he was going to do something stupid there. Why would you tell him something that would make him so angry?" Cindy asked.

I arched my eyebrows and breathed deeply, trying to calm the frantic beats of my heart. "I knew that he wasn't going to let this go. I had to tell him something that would actually put him off me. Ever since we started going out Mark has always been jealous. He's always been insecure that someone would tempt me away from him. I think that's what drove his anger, you know, almost as though he was punishing me for betraying him even though it hadn't happened yet. But whenever he caught men looking at me he flew into a rage and somehow blamed me for it. I had to say something that would put him off me. I think I'm tainted for him now. Whenever he thinks of me he'll never be able to forget the image of me with another man, so hopefully I'll never hear from him again."

"Hopefully, but I wouldn't bet on it. He's fucking crazy. Let's get your stuff and get out of here," Cindy said. We walked through the house and quickly packed up my things. I was glad to see that Mark hadn't damaged anything of mine in a furious rage. I was probably spared that since he knew if he didn't show restraint it would be another reason why I wouldn't return to him. This place had been a big part of my life, but I wasn't sorry to leave. It only reminded me of how I had wasted my years and that there were better things out there for me.

I left feeling stronger than ever before, and ready to embrace the future in a way that I never had before. It had always been a bleak, foreboding thing, but right now it gleamed with hope and I was eager to see what it held in store for me.

*

One evening I was sitting in Cindy's apartment. She had gone out dancing and invited me along, but I declined on this occasion because I wanted some time to myself. I had my laptop out and the screen was filled with different tabs showing various parts of the world. There were so many wonderful places that all offered so many different things it was impossible to know where to begin. There were modern cities that offered glamour and excitement, or rustic areas that were steeped in history and culture. For the first time ever the world opened up to me, as though a flower had bloomed and had its beauty on full display. Usually I was locked in the mindset of dreaming about things that I could never do, but this time it was all possible, and I was cursed with the burden of choice.

My phone buzzed. I was tempted to ignore it because Mark was still sending me messages and calling me occasionally, but I glanced towards the screen and was intrigued to see Jack's name appear. He was about the last person I expected to call, and I wondered what he wanted. Perhaps one night hadn't been enough and he was willing to pay for another. Spikes of pleasure lanced through me as memories of the night we shared came back in their glorious fury. I wouldn't have been opposed to a second round. I leaned back in my chair and answered in a sultry tone.

"Mr. Easter, I'm surprised to hear from you, but delighted none the less. What can I do for you?"

"Sandi... good... are you still in the country?" he asked. I frowned. There was something different about his voice, although I couldn't quite pinpoint it over the phone.

"Yeah I am, is there something on your mind?"

"Can we see each other again?" he asked.

"Sure thing. At the same rate as before?" I teased, laughing lightly as the words left my mouth.

"I just... I want to talk. My Dad died."

The words dropped like a stone and all the playfulness died within me. I suddenly felt awkward and guilty, and now I realized what the strange tone in his voice had been; grief.

Chapter Eighteen

I hadn't thought of Jack as the kind of man to be vulnerable to emotions. He gave the impression of being able to carry any burden or able to meet any challenge, but when I saw him again he looked as though he hadn't slept for a week. Stubble peppered his jaw and his hair was unkempt, freed of its styled gloss. His shoulders were slumped and there was an aura of defeat around him, as though he had been bested by some vicious creature. We met outside, near the harbor. Skyscrapers towered above us, and the city thrummed with life behind us. The sea stretched out for an eternity, glittering under the bright sun. People were dotted along a grassy area, sharing picnics and relaxing with books. When I arrived Jack was sitting gazing out to sea, a man who was lost in his own thoughts. I wasn't even sure why out of everyone in the world he had called me, but I found I couldn't resist his plea for companionship. There was a part of it that was just being a decent human being of course, but I couldn't ignore the connection between us either. I hadn't been able to stop thinking about him since we spent the night together, and I wondered if there had been a chance for things to work out between us in another life.

"Jack, I'm so sorry about what happened," I said as I lowered myself down to the soft, warm grass.

"Thank you," he said, his voice gravelly, his words heavy with the weight of emotion. "And thank you for coming. I know that we said we wouldn't see each other again but..."

"I have to admit I was surprised to receive your call. Isn't there someone else you'd rather speak with? Someone who knows you better?"

Jack wore a wry smile. He reached down and ripped out a few blades of grass from the ground, before scattering them away. "The funny thing is that not many people know me all that well. Dad was the one who knew me best, but now he's... well... he's gone. And when

I looked at all the people in my life I realized that I didn't have anyone close to me. They were all business associates or employees. I didn't have anyone I could actually share my emotions with. I spent so much time building up this rigorous routine and isolating myself so that I could focus on my work that I didn't make time for anything else, and I had nobody to open up to. You were the only one I could think of. I'm sorry. I know you probably don't want this burden but I just... I just needed someone to talk to."

"Of course Jack. It's perfectly natural," I said, although I did wonder how a man could make it to this point in his life without having a firm network of friends. But Jack did say he was devoted to his job. "Do you want to tell me about him?"

"I don't even know where to begin. He was this larger than life character. Wherever he went he got people's attention, and he always seemed to know what to do. From a young age I knew that I wanted to be exactly like him, and that nothing was going to stop me. But I think I learned the wrong lessons. He tried to tell me something before he died, that I should open myself up to other possibilities, but I didn't listen, just like I never listened. I only ever focused on improving the performance of our companies and accumulating more assets."

"You must have made a few friends along the way though?" I asked.

Jack laughed. He turned towards me and ran his tongue along his teeth. "Have you looked me up on the Internet?" he asked.

"I haven't," I said.

"I think you should. You can see what people say about me."

He turned his gaze back towards the sea as I pulled out my cell. I opened the web browser and typed in his name. I was shocked when I saw the plethora of articles and opinion pieces that appeared in response to this search. Most of them were inflammatory and painted Jack as a villain for buying out any company that showed the slightest hint of being able to compete with his, or being ruthless enough to patent technology that they weren't going to use, just to prevent others from profiting off of it. To read these articles was to learn about a man who showed no mercy in business and who had no qualms or morals about crushing the hopes and dreams of people who were trying to make something of themselves. I wondered which Jack was the real one. Was it the tender, kind, charming man I had gotten to know, or was it this villain?

"Why would you show me this Jack?"

"I thought you'd want to see the real me. This is why I don't have anyone to confide in. I'm not a popular man. I devoted myself to the company a long time ago, vowing to make it bigger and better than ever before, and I achieved that. But along the way I lost something as well. I wasn't even aware of it until recently... until you."

"Me?"

"I thought I didn't need to be with anyone Sandi. I thought I didn't need to feel connected with anyone, but then you came along. I thought one night was enough. One night should have been enough, but I'm not sure it was. And now you're the only person in the world I can talk to about this. Isn't that sad? I'm in my thirties and there's nobody who likes me enough to be my friend. There's nobody I can share my inner thoughts with. I thought that at some point I could change the circumstances of my life and follow Dad's advice, but I think it's going to be harder than I thought it would be."

"What advice was it exactly?"

"Dad told me to find someone to share life with. I think he was trying to tell me that it was lonely at the top, and if I didn't have someone to share the burden it would wreck me. I didn't believe him at first, but it's only now that I realize he was the one I shared the burden with. Now I don't have him and I... I feel lost."

His voice cracked with emotion. A hand rose to wipe an errant tear away from his eyes.

"I'm really sorry this happened Jack, but you'll pull through it. I know it doesn't seem like it at the moment, but things get better.

They always do. And you're only in your thirties. You still have time to change. Is this the way you want to be remembered?" I asked, holding up the phone.

"I don't know anymore. At the funeral there were so many people there for Dad, and I can't help but wonder what mine is going to be like. The way it's going I'm expecting people to come to spit on my grave," he laughed, but it was a laugh devoid of humor.

"I've thought about my funeral a lot too," I said. "I don't think I'd have anyone turn up. I haven't made any connections in life either Jack. I grew up in an orphanage and it only hurt to have feelings and friendships with other people because they eventually moved on and moved away. I don't know what it's like to lose a parent because I never had any to lose, but I do know what it's like to be alone and to be lost in the world."

"How do you cope with it?"

"Not very well," I said, running a hand through my hair. "The first time I came to the city I wanted to reconnect with someone who meant a lot to me. I found him but he... he'd changed. He looked at me as though I didn't exist, and then he pretended that we had never met. I'd never felt so alone. Then I met Mark and I guess I just... I stayed with him because I was afraid to live life by myself. I thought that anything was better than being alone. But now I know that it's not. Look, I don't know what you're like as a businessman, but this stuff isn't the Jack I've gotten to know, and I'm sure it's not the only part of you."

"It's the only part that people see."

"Then show them something different. Maybe your legacy doesn't have to be in creating this super company that owns the world, it could be in setting up trust funds and foundations to help people who don't have the means to help themselves, it could be in using your wealth to make the world a better place. You have the means to do anything Jack, all you have to do is decide what it is that you want to do. Hell, you changed my life. If you can do that you can do anything."

Jack smirked. "I don't think I can keep going around paying people to spend the night with me."

I blushed and tapped my fingers against my thigh. "You know you didn't have to pay me, right? I mean, I'm not complaining, but it's not like you had to force me to spend the night with you."

"I don't know. I told you that I wanted to pay you because I don't have time to go through the routine of a relationship, but the truth is that I'm afraid I've forgotten what to do. It's been so long now. I feel like I've isolated myself to such an extent that I don't know how to exist in the world anymore."

"You don't feel that way with me."

He turned to look at me and the way his gaze penetrated me was almost as powerful as when our bodies had been linked.

"You're different. I don't know what it is, but you just are. I think I've felt it from the moment we first met."

"Maybe it's because I haven't been brought up in the world like other people. I've always been alone. I was always passed over, forgotten, and ignored. In a way it's as though I haven't actually lived at all yet."

"That sounds sad, but I know how you feel. When you were talking about all the things you would do with money it made me realize how little I had done. I always thought I had to be focused on a single thing, but even then Dad was disappointed. I always thought he wanted me to give everything I had to the family business, and now I realize that's not enough."

"What do you think he'd want from you?"

"He'd want me to have a family," Jack said.

"I think it's nice to have someone thinking about you and wanting you to live up to a certain ideal. I don't have any idea of the type of person I'm supposed to be. Nobody has ever hoped or expected me to be anything. You still have plenty of time to make your father proud Jack. It's never too late to change."

Jack nodded as he digested my words. "So what are you planning to do now? Have you decided what you're going to do with the money?"

"I'm going to invest some of it, and then I think I'm going to use the rest to go traveling. I feel like there's so much to see out there it would almost be wrong not to go traveling. I just don't know where to go. The problem with there being so many places to see is that it's difficult to make a choice."

When Jack spoke again his voice was low and quiet. "What if you stayed here for a little while? Until you decided I mean. Would that be so bad?"

"Jack I... I don't have that much holding me here."

"What if you did? I was thinking Sandi... what if we spent a little bit more time together? I know there's something between us. I told myself that we were just going to spend one night together, but I haven't been able to stop thinking about you. If it is time for a change in my life then I think that you might be that change. Maybe... maybe we could go out on a few dates and see if there's something there?"

Jack looked deeply in my eyes and for a moment I felt as though I could gaze into his soul. My heart pitched when he asked me because before he had been adamant that he wouldn't have the time or the space in his life for romance. But grief could do strange things to people. I thought about it for a few moments. Staying went against everything I had vowed to myself, and yet I couldn't deny the temptation of going out with him. To know that he had been unable to stop thinking of me in the same way as I had been unable to stop thinking about him was incredible. In his eyes I wasn't some forlorn orphan who had no business in the world; I was a woman who could connect with his soul. But then again I had shown bad judgment with men in the past and I wasn't sure if I should let history repeat itself.

"Jack I'm really flattered but I just don't know. I mean, I feel the same way about you, but I haven't had the best experience with men. I've just reached a point in my life where I feel ready to take a big leap, and I don't know if I'm willing to pass that opportunity up for the sake of being with someone else. I'm just not sure it's the right time for me to go after something like this again."

I hated the words as I said them, but I was afraid to let myself be open to love when it had never been kind to me in the past.

"Then how about we make a compromise?" he suggested. "While you're figuring out what to do with your life how about we spend some time together and see what happens? It might just happen that all this talk is for nothing."

I had the feeling that he didn't believe what he was saying. I wasn't sure I believed it either. Even then, sitting on the grass in this innocuous manner there was a prickling heat between us. Whether it was a mistake or not I didn't know at the time, but I found myself nodding and giving into the temptation.

"Are you sure you can make room for me in your schedule?" I asked, half-jokingly. He nodded and his eyes sparkled. I felt heat rising to the surface of my skin and I wondered if this was an adventure that was more exciting than what the world could offer.

Chapter Nineteen

Cindy was no less surprised than I was that I had stayed, but at first I was certain it was the right decision. Although Jack was still weighed down by his grief he was good company and we bounced off each other well. When we were together it was easy to forget that we were from different worlds. We shared a good rapport and the chemistry between us was impossible to deny. Given that he shared his misgivings about romance with me I was surprised when he was utterly charming and didn't put a foot wrong. Our first few weeks together were filled with meals and trips to the theatre and visits to expensive bars. I bought some new glamorous outfits and enjoyed shopping in a certain standard of store that I had never been able to visit before.

I was filled with excitement, feeling as though I had finally been unleashed on the world without having to compromise anything. I had planned a list of things for us to do, things that had never been on my radar. It felt as though I had rediscovered a part of myself that I had lost over the years and I was beginning to think that I had made the right decision to stay with him. After all, I figured, it wasn't as though I had to travel right this instance, and it would probably be more fun traveling with him as well.

One night we were hanging out at his apartment and I gazed out at the stars. He was playing some classical music. It was one of his attempts to expose me to something he thought was precious and wonderful about the world. I was scrolling through my phone, looking at various places when suddenly I was struck by an idea.

"Shall we take a trip?" I asked. "We could fly anywhere in the world, just leave right now without any hesitation."

"Right now?" he said. From the wary tone in his voice I could tell that he wasn't as enthused as I was.

"Yeah, why not? The night is young, the stars are dancing in the sky, we could seize this opportunity and go anywhere we want. I was thinking we could try flying to Rome. Europe has been tempting me, and Rome seems like it has a lot of things to see and do."

"I'm sure we can get to Rome at some point, but I don't think we should just go out there now."

"Why not? What's stopping us? There's nothing wrong with a bit of spontaneity."

"I have a meeting tomorrow. It's a shareholder meeting so I can't skip it."

I pouted. Apparently every meeting was one that he couldn't skip. "Okay," I sighed. "Well, how about we take a trip to Disneyworld at the weekend? I thought we could fly down and just rush around the park to see how much we could do, make a challenge out of it."

"I don't know, that place is always crowded and filled with kids. I know what might be fun; we could go up in the mountains and stay in a cabin. It's quiet and peaceful, although we can't go this weekend. I have some reports that I need to read. But I'm sure I could fit it in the following weekend."

"Sure," I said, my heart sinking. I was certain that something would likely come up the following weekend as well. I had begun to notice a pattern too, and I decided to test it. "Jack, what about going to a new nightclub over the weekend? I can always ask Cindy where the best place to go is. Blake would know."

"I don't know, being locked in a place with loads of other people isn't my idea of fun. You can go if you like though."

That was a step up from how Mark used to react, but I couldn't help but feel that something was wrong. "Is there anything you want to do that doesn't involve us sitting around here?" I asked.

Jack looked across at me with a frown on his face. "What about the zoo?" he suggested.

"The zoo?!" I huffed and folded my arms across my chest.

"What's wrong with the zoo? I like animals."

"I like animals too, but a zoo isn't the most exciting place I can think of, and I don't really like the idea of having to schedule these trips with each other. I thought that we could live more spontaneously than that and do far grander things. Hell, I got to go to the zoo when I was in the orphanage! Is that really the best you can come up with?" My voice rose even though I did not intend it to, but fear was beginning to tinge my words.

Jack straightened his posture. The music that played lowered and became more dramatic, as though it could sense the shift in mood between us.

"Not every day has to be filled with some kind of excitement Sandi," his words were carried with a huffed breath, as though I was asking the impossible.

"I'm not asking for that. I just want us to be able to go out and have fun. I want to enjoy life, which is what you promised we'd do when I decided to stay here."

"Are you saying that you regret your choice?"

"No! No... at least I don't think so I just... I want to feel that I'm taking part in the world. I want to be out there experiencing things, not stuck up here looking down on it. Don't think I haven't noticed how much you're giving to your work. You said that you were going to ease off. There are other people that can do your job Jack. Your problem is that you can't let go of control, and I'm starting to think that even if you want to change it's impossible for you to do so."

"I have changed Sandi, but you can't just expect me to walk away from everything I've built. That's not fair."

"I'm not asking that of you. I'm just trying to make you see that there's a way to have balance in your life. There are moments when you've been so sweet and romantic to me that I can't imagine how lucky I've become, but then there are times when you treat me like an afterthought. I don't want to live in a world where everything is set to a routine and where we have to put aside what we want to do because there are other responsibilities. Christ, you have all the freedom in the world to do whatever you want and all you want to do is work! You said that you wanted to be with me, but now you have me you can't escape your routine. I don't want to live like this."

"What are you saying?" he scrunched up his face.

"I don't know. I just... I thought it would be different, that's all," I said, turning away from him.

Jack rose from the couch and walked to the window. He stood with his back to me, clasping his hands behind his back. He stared out at the night sky. "Maybe I was right and I'm not suited to romance."

"All you have to do is change Jack. I was with a man for a long time who kept telling me we couldn't do things, or that I couldn't do things, and I don't want that to happen again. I just don't understand why you're so wedded to your company when there are so many other people who could handle things. You have assistants and managers and other executives. You're not the only person in the world who can do this. There are other people. All you have to do is let go and let them take control."

"This is my family's work," Jack said, his words laced with a spiteful edge. "It's all I have left. All they've worked for is entirely down to me now. I have to make sure it succeeds. I'm the one who has driven the success of this company. It is my birthright and if I let someone else take control it's going to plummet. I can't trust anyone else with it."

Each word was like a coffin in the nail of our relationship. My heart sank and I sighed quietly, feeling the weight of despair and regret anchoring my soul. Perhaps I had been too eager in pursuing a relationship with Jack. I had let myself be blind to the warning signs that had blared in the back of my mind.

"Jack, your life and your company are two different things. But with your company there are other people who can take care of it. With your life there's only you. If you neglect it then you're never going to understand what else is out there in the world. I just don't get you. I spent my whole life dreaming of being a part of something greater than myself, of getting out in the world and experiencing it all. I used to sit in that orphanage and listen to the stories of the kids who passed through, leeching off their experiences as though I was some kind of vampire. But I never had any of them for myself. And now I'm at a point when I finally thought I could have some, but you're too busy working to enjoy life. You don't see the opportunities you have or how lucky you are. I just feel trapped again and I don't want to feel like that anymore."

"You can't seriously be comparing me to Mark," Jack said as he turned around sharply, spitting out Mark's name with utter disgust. Of course he wasn't the same in that he didn't hit me, but there were all different kinds of abuse and one of them was control. Jack kept denying me the opportunity to do things. I was willing to give him some leeway at first, but when it started to become a pattern I knew that I didn't want to suffer in a similar relationship again. I was not willing to sacrifice such a part of myself for the sake of a man.

"I'm not Jack. But there are certain things I feel are similar. I don't like that you never make spending time with me a priority. I don't like that whenever I have an idea of something we could do together you always end up saying no, and then we either stay here or we do something you're comfortable with. This is supposed to be my life, but I feel like I never get to do anything I want to do. I don't mean to sound spoiled I just... I have to be careful to not make the same mistakes. I don't want my life to be defined by being restrained. I don't want to feel trapped all the time. I just... I just need to think about where my life is going and what I need to do. I'm sorry."

Without saying anything else and without giving him a chance to respond I rose from the couch and glided out of his apartment. The elevator ride to the bottom was a long one, and by the time it descended to the bottom tears stained my cheeks. Arguments could rise so easily from nothing. All it took was one surge of emotion and suddenly one conversation had a violent edge to it, leaving behind a wake of destruction. I wasn't sure what was going to happen next or what the future held for me and Jack. I just knew that I couldn't let myself feel confined by a man, no matter what. I worried that the blazing heat of our night together was just a sizzling, random occurrence and that we could not sustain a relationship. The time we spent together was good, but it was the time apart that was the problem. I was tired of being second best. I deserved to be more than that. I wasn't just going to stand by and let myself fall into another grim routine where I was forced to be less than myself again.

This was going to be the era of Sandi, and I wasn't going to let anything else get in the way. That's what I told myself anyway, but I certainly didn't feel defiant as tears poured down my cheeks. When I called Cindy to tell her what happened my words were barely intelligible through the disparate sobs that cascaded out of me in a torrent.

Chapter Twenty

I stood by the window, watching the door close behind her. Sandi had just left in a swirl of emotion while I stood stoically by the window, just as I had done all my life. It felt as though the world had always been spinning around me and I was in the midst of it all, locked into a destiny that I thought was my prison, and yet was Sandi correct? Had I voluntarily condemned myself to this fate?

I had been honest with her throughout our time together, and this event was a replay of so many other moments during my life when a neglected lover had marched away from me. Except this time it was different. This time I didn't want Sandi to leave. I had tried my hardest to be the man I thought she wanted. I had tried to scale back my involvement in the company, but it was so difficult when it was all I had ever known. Sandi was a wild child, wanting to do this and that and explore the world. Sometimes it sounded exhausting, but every time she suggested this I thought about what might happen to the company in my absence.

It didn't help that the company was all I had left of Dad either. Was I just supposed to let it all fade away into the past?

The past... I had always been so concerned with the past. It had defined every decision I ever made. I wanted to make sure that I remained in the annals of history along with my ancestors, that I continued their legacy, but Sandi was right. If I gave so much of myself to them, then what was going to be left for me? Who was going to be left to mourn me? And if I didn't give up some control of the company I was never going to have a son to leave the company too.

But could I change now even though I had been stuck in this habit for such a long time?

I hated how Sandi had compared me to Mark. I knew the world didn't look favorably upon me, but I thought I was different with Sandi. It was a shock to hear that I made her feel confined or restricted.

All I ever wanted was for her to be happy, and now that she was gone I felt her absence keenly. I remembered what Dad said about finding someone to trust and confide in. The more I thought about him the more I pictured him outside of work. He always made time for Mom, and their marriage was never anything but strong. When I spoke to her as she was dying she said that she had no regrets, and that if she could do it all over again she would have. Dad had made her life worth living.

I wanted to do the same for Sandi.

I chastised myself for being so stupid. The world hated me, but somehow Sandi had seen through that. She was trying to help me become a better person and make me see that I didn't have to continue defining myself the way I always had been. And I had just pushed her away, like I had with everyone else.

Well, this time I wasn't going to fall into old habits and I wasn't going to let the world be right about me. I just had to think about how I could convince Sandi to stay. It was time for me to make a choice between managing the company and managing my life.

*

I stood outside Sandi's house. It was the first time I had ever made a gesture like this. My heart thumped in my chest and I hoped that I wouldn't be summarily turned away. The world might have seen me as a villain, but I didn't care about that. All that mattered to me was how I looked in Sandi's eyes. I had planned something that I hoped would alleviate any of the concerns she had about me, but I also told myself that if she turned me away I wouldn't try and convince her otherwise. I had to respect her decision. It was the first step of me not treating this as another business deal. I couldn't just negotiate for better terms or brute force my way into getting what I wanted. My car stood behind me, sleek and black, with the driver waiting to take us away. I wore a blue shirt and grey pants, hoping that by appearing casual I would give her the impression that I was ready to set aside my life as a businessman for her.

Sandi appeared at the door, holding onto it as though it were a shield. I could see the doubt in her eyes, the hesitancy, the fear that if she let me back into her life she would be repeating the mistakes of the past. She had opened up to me about her relationship with Mark. I knew how deeply it affected her and the last thing I wanted was to be another problem in her life, another source of trauma. She crossed her arms and looked at me defiantly.

"What are you doing here Jack?" she asked. I stepped forward, opening my palms to her and tilting forward slightly, as though she was a queen and I was but a lowly lord offering my respect.

"I'm here to win you back Sandi. I'm here to convince you that I'm worth another shot."

"I've been thinking about it Jack and I just don't know. I've given too many people too many shots in life. I've been thinking that I should take a leaf out of your book actually and be more ruthless."

"You don't want to do that," I said. The bluntness of my words took her by surprise. She recoiled, and I immediately backtracked. "I don't mean to tell you what you should or shouldn't do, I just mean that being ruthless hasn't gotten me anywhere in life, not in the ways that matter. I've been thinking long and hard about myself and the way I live my life, and I know I want things to change. I never meant to push you away Sandi. I never meant to make you feel less than anything important. I think I didn't realize how hard it was going to be for me to break out of old habits. For such a long time I associated my wellbeing with the company, but I realize now how toxic a relationship that was. I let it cloud my judgment in other matters and I just couldn't let go when I needed to. When you came back into my life I should have given you more time, and I'm just sorry that it took you walking away for me to see what I needed to do to make things change."

I could sense that she wanted to believe me, but there was still so much holding her back. I just wanted to take her in my arms and convince her with a kiss, but I knew I needed to do more than that. I knew I needed to be patient. This wasn't something I could rush. I had been waiting for her for a lifetime. I could wait a little longer.

"Jack, it's all well and good you saying this, but I've heard words like these before. I wish I could take you at your word, but I can't. I know that might not be fair of me, but I need more."

"Then you'll have more," I said, flashing her a smirk. "I've booked us tickets to Rome. They leave tonight. We're staying in a reputable hotel and I haven't booked any return tickets, meaning that we can stay there as long as we like, or even move on to another European country. It's an open ended trip without any routine or agenda. We'll just fly out there and see where the wind takes us."

Sandi's face flickered with excitement, but still there was something holding her back. "Jack, that's a wonderful gesture, but how do I know this is going to last? What if something happens and your company comes calling? How do I know you won't just drop everything and return here?"

"I've taken care of that as well." I reached into my pocket and pulled out a sheet of paper, handing it over to her. I watched her eyes flick across the paper as she read the words, and then understanding spread over her face.

"Jack this... what have you done?"

"I've done what I should have done a long time ago. I still maintain a controlling stake in the company, but I'm stepping back from the day to day running of it. You were right. There are plenty of other people who can handle the company. I've just been too scared to let it go because I haven't had anything else. But now I have you. Now, if things truly do get bad I might have to step back in, but I've hired good people over the years and I need to trust them. I need to trust myself as well, trust that I can find some other meaning in life. When you walked away

I felt awful and empty. I didn't want to let you go. I don't want you to feel like you're trapped with me. I want us to enrich each others' lives."

I spoke sincerely and I hoped she welcomed my words.

She stared at the piece of paper I had given her for what seemed like an eternity. There was a horrible moment when I thought she was going to tell me that this wasn't enough, that she wanted to take a break from relationships entirely. I thought of how disappointed my father would have been that I hadn't been able to follow the advice he had given me.

But then her face lit up and she rushed towards me, flinging her arms around my neck. I gathered her into my arms and vowed to myself that I would never let her go. As important as the company was to me, as important as legacy was, I couldn't hold it in my arms nor could I feel the love in return. I had fooled myself all these years into thinking that I didn't need anyone, but as I held Sandi close to me I knew what my father had been trying to tell me. I knew something that all my ancestors had known as well.

I hoped one day I would be able to pass it on to my children, but that was still far away into the future.

Chapter Twenty One

The air in Italy was warm. We stood on the porch of our hotel. It overlooked the beautiful city. I couldn't see any towering skyscrapers, and the light wasn't drowned out by the brilliance of electric lights. In the distance I could see the Colosseum, lit up in a blue and purple hue. Elsewhere in Rome was the Vatican. Religion and history collided in this wonderful place. The buildings were imbued with a sense of history and I felt humbled just by being in this place.

I was also humbled by the gestures of love that Jack had shown me as well. He had torn asunder all my doubts and left me certain that he was the man for me. The fact that he would actually step back from his responsibilities in his company for my sake warmed my heart and gave me confidence that he wasn't going to be another Mark. I might have said a few harsh words to Jack. There were still a lot of things left for us to figure out, but I was grateful to be given the opportunity to learn about life together. I had come a long way from being a lonely, broken-hearted orphan wondering if I would ever find my place in the world. Now I was sitting with a billionaire, drinking fine wine and eating the juiciest strawberries I had ever tasted. I was in one of the most beautiful cities in the world and I had no idea what was going to come next, and I loved it. It felt as though anything could happen, and I was eager to explore it all.

"So I was speaking to the concierge and he told me that there's an underground party we could go to, if I tip him enough money," Jack said.

I wore a slanted smile and chuckled. "Jack, you don't have to keep making these suggestions. I'm not completely a wild child. Being in Rome is almost an adventure enough."

"Okay, just so long as I get credit for being willing to go to a party."

"You have credit. I won't forget it," I assured him. We laughed lightly and spent a moment just gazing at each other. The feelings that had grown between us were genuine. I think they had always been there, even from the first moment he had walked into the massage parlor. But I had always felt a sense of inferiority. It was only now that I felt an equal to him, as though I belonged in his world.

"You know, I do want to speak to you about some of your business interests though. I think more could be done to help the world and the people in it. Not everything has to be done with this cold ruthlessness that you're so famous for," I said. Jack nodded and dabbed some strawberry juice away from his lips.

"I know, I know, and I have been thinking about a number of things. Actually I came up with one idea that you might like. I thought about what you told me, about how lonely it was for you in the orphanage and how you always felt like you were alone. I think that perhaps we should make a donation to the orphanage and try and improve the lives of the people who live there. Perhaps we could create a program to prepare them for life in the outside world. As you said, it must have been difficult for you when you had nobody to turn to."

My heart swelled with love as what he suggested was a compassionate thing, and something that was sorely needed.

"That sounds great."

"I thought you could run this fund or whatever it's going to become, too."

"Me? But I have no experience in business," I said, wondering if he had gone too far in his estimation of my abilities.

"There are plenty of people who have experience in business so there will be no difficulty in finding you an advisor, but you know what needs to be done. You know what these kids are going to need. I can't think of anyone better to head up this endeavor."

"It would be a good venture to help people," I agreed, already having made the decision to follow through with his plans. I had never thought of myself doing something this important before, but it felt natural. If I could prevent other people from going through what I had been through then I knew that I would be able to die knowing that I had made a difference in the world. I thought about other things I could do as well, like open a shelter for survivors of domestic abuse too, and perhaps even counseling to help those who struggled with anger issues. There were so many ideas, and I felt excited about pursuing them. But there was something else I wanted to talk to Jack about as well. So far we had skirted around talking about the future because there had been so many things in the present to occupy our minds, but it seemed time to put some of these matters to rest.

"Jack, there's something that's been playing on my mind. It's about the future. Our future," I said, venturing a glance towards him. He gazed at me intently, waiting for me to elaborate. "I know that legacy is important to you, and I'm not opposed to having my own biological children, but I think I'd also like to adopt as well. I just know that there are so many kids out there who feel unwanted and lonely. I hate to think of them feeling that nobody is ever going to choose them."

Jack looked at me thoughtfully. I could tell that there was something on his mind. It was rare that he was hesitant with his words, but he seemed to struggle with this, and I was soon to find out why.

"Can I ask you a question Sandi?"

"Of course," I said. It always seemed that whenever a question needed permission to be asked it was an awkward one, so I steeled myself against whatever this was going to be.

"Well, you go on a lot about not having anyone around in your life to count on and how you've always been lonely. I was just wondering if you've thought about changing that, considering that now you have a lot more resources. I mean, it's possible that we could find your biological parents, if that's something that would interest you?"

My heart clutched and an uneasy feeling settled in my stomach. It had been a long time since I'd thought about my parents, but I couldn't deny that I had wondered about them. Who wouldn't in my position?

"Have you ever tried to find them?" he asked.

I exhaled deeply, trying to calm my heart. "I thought about it once, a long time ago. I figured that maybe if I found them the rest of my life would make sense. But they were the ones that gave me up. If they wanted me around they would have kept me. All I got from them was suffering, and I didn't think any answers I'd be given would change that. I've been alone in this world for a reason and if I went chasing ghosts of the past I'd never be able to be happy. I don't think there's anything I could learn from them that would make it worth the pain. I just want to make sure that nobody else has to go through what I went through."

*

We spoke for hours, revealing the deepest layers of our hearts. Candles lit the bedroom. Shadows danced as we retreated inside with the promise of intimacy in our eyes. We had shared our secrets with each other and now it was time to share a little more. He took my hand and led me to the bed. It was a comforting gesture, and I felt safe with him. I was wearing a loose, light dress that rippled like waves under his touch. A gasp left my mouth as his hands curled around my waist and I started to feel the all too familiar stirrings of lust again. My lips parted and my eyes closed. I sank into a wonderful kiss, and felt all the angles of his body pressing against me.

Our chests rose as we gazed into each others' eyes. We had been intimate before, but now it felt as though we had shed all the doubts and the concerns that had held our hearts back from loving each other purely and completely. I tasted the strawberries on his lips. Shadows danced upon our bodies as we undressed each other. The musky smell of aroused sweat lingered around us, as though we were caught in a miasma of heat. I wrapped my arms around his trunk of a body, my fingers deftly plying his taut flesh. It was the same flesh I had massaged when we had been strangers. I had become an expert of his body before I became an expert of his soul, and I used all my skills to make him purr.

He relinquished his strength and sank to the bed as I draped myself over him, dragging my fingers all over his body. I undid the knots in his muscles and teased the secret sweet spots. It was as though I plucked a note from guitar strings, such was the response I received from him. Small moans and grunts emerged from his throat. I could feel him melt underneath my prompting fingers.

I dragged my nails down the back of his thighs and got him to turn around, gazing in awe at every inch of his body. I knew I would never tire of it. The sight of his masculinity made something burn inside me. I pressed my hand against the narrowing thatch of hair that ran down the middle of his stomach to his thighs. A hunger gnawed in the back of my throat. I smiled and licked my lips as I took him in my hands, twisting and twirling my fingers to make him shudder. I slowly lowered myself down. My hair grazed his thighs as I kissed the tip of his manhood and then lowered my hand to the base of his shaft, plunging him into my mouth as I did so. Wet and warm, I felt his body respond underneath me. I could feel the tremors quaking through him and I felt such a sense of pride that I could make a billionaire act this way. We were opposites in some ways, but in all the ways that mattered we were the same.

I sucked deep and slow, resting my tongue flat against the base of his shaft before I drew myself up, bringing a line of saliva back with me. His manhood glistened beautifully, as though it had been sculpted by the gods, and I knew I was fortunate to be blessed with the ability to caress him. Heat radiated from him, as well. I breathed in his deep aroma, getting ever more intoxicated with every breath. I gifted him soft kisses before sucking him once again. I could feel the tension rise within him, and then I released his erection and knelt beside him, tucking my legs under my body.

I took his hand and kissed his palm, murmuring as I slid my tongue around his fingers, bringing them into my mouth too. Then I arched my neck back and forced his hand around my neck and down my chest, encouraging him to rest against my breasts. I felt so small with his giant hands around me, as though he was a god encompassing the world in his palm. He squeezed and stroked and my nipples immediately hardened. Waves of pleasure surged through me, emanating from a hidden core that radiated out in a scorching wave. A smiled played upon my lips and a delighted laugh left my mouth as I felt him play with my supple skin. His fingers sank into my soft curves and pinched my nipples, blurring pain with pleasure in a sweet cocktail. I rocked back and forth, biting my lower lip as I braced myself against the pleasure. I squirmed as well, already feeling the hot wetness simmering between my thighs. I playfully pushed his hand down and opened my legs. The smile faded from my face, replaced by a wide oval as I felt the heaven of his touch against me. Just a caress of his fingers was enough to make me shiver, but of course he was not going to torture me by just giving me that.

His fingers curled against me, fighting against the wetness. I groaned as I felt him slide slowly inside me. My eyelids fluttered shut as my heart was opened and all the pleasure began to flow through. I was surprised that it could happen this instantly and this dramatically, but it was as though it had been building up inside me for a life time and Jack had the ability to shepherd it out, as though he was a matador controlling a stampeding bull. Hair fell across my face like a veil and I felt it cover my mouth. I shifted my body so that Jack could get even deeper inside me. I glanced down and saw his fingers locked in my body, so intimate, so close, as though we had been less than complete before we found each other.

My hand ran down his body and toyed with him again, feeling the hardness twitching in my palm. Sweat prickled on his chest and neck. I felt crystal beads drip down my collarbone and rest in the hollow of my throat. In that moment I knew it didn't matter what I did with the rest of my life; I just knew that I had to be with him. I leaned down and pressed my lips against his. The kiss was soft and sweet, tender and yearning. Our breaths danced and swirled in the air, becoming one. The same was true of our heartbeats. When I kissed him it was as though I was giving him a part of myself, as though I was surrendering myself to him, and him to me.

I tightened my grip on him and felt him moan. His hand reached up and brushed the hair away from my face, curling around the back of my head. When he looked at me I felt special. When he told me he loved me I was born anew. I wasn't just some orphan to him, and he wasn't just some billionaire to me.

We were going to change the world together.

We had already changed ourselves.

He rose to his knees and took my hands. I could feel my dampness on his fingers, and his arousal pressing against me. We kissed deeply again, romantically, illuminated by the soft glow of the candles. He gazed in awe at my feminine beauty, as I was entranced by his masculine aura. He sat down, resting against the headboard, and pulled me onto him. Our movements were graceful and elegant, as though we were performing some ethereal dance that had already been ordained. Every moment with him felt as though it had been fated to be, and I was not going to go to war with the cosmos. Our mouths met again in a heavenly kiss. At the same time our bodies slid together. A shimmering, blissful haze fell upon us as we met in the most intimate way possible. Suddenly he was me and I was him. I clung to him and his arms wrapped me up like vines, as though I was entombed in his love.

We kissed deeply as we made love. He rested a hand against the base of my spine. His hips moved smoothly and forcefully, as though he was in control of everything. Waves of pleasure flowed through me, growing and rising in their intensity. I buried myself in his neck and then he tugged at my hair, arching my neck back, kissing me all over my chest and breasts. Our skin was alive with pleasure. Our hearts beat as one. We moved in harmony and I knew that I could lose myself in him forever. I nibbled on his lip playfully and then pressed my forehead against his, wishing I could tell him in words how much I wanted him and how much he did to me, but I trusted that my body conveyed everything he needed to know.

I closed my eyes and gasped out the surging songs of passion that could not be contained within me. The rhythm of his body tore them out of my soul and I let them fly free, soaring through the air on an orgasmic wave. I leaned against him like a pillar as my body grew weak, as the strength was drained from me with this constant flow of ecstasy that flooded in a torrent out of me. The world was more vivid than it had ever been before. I was more alive than I had ever been before, and it was all because of Jack.

I could never have guessed how much my life would change when he came into the massage parlor and asked me for a happy ending. I could never have imagined how tender a man's touch could be when compared with the rough hits I had taken over the years, and I was so glad in myself that I had trusted that Jack would not be the same as Mark. It finally felt as though I had escaped my past and I could embrace my future, a future that was going to be entirely different to what came before. Tears of happiness flowed down my cheeks mixing with the sweat as we made love. I don't think Jack noticed, but I couldn't keep my emotions in. I loved him, I trusted him, and I knew that he wasn't going to up and leave me. I knew I wasn't going to have to be alone.

More tremors surged through me, but this time I knew they were his. His warmth flowed inside me, slick and lustrous. I murmured my delight as I held him while he shuddered, the powerful orgasm seizing his body in a thunderous storm. He held me tightly, kissing me softly. I wiped the tears from my eyes and laughed.

"Why are you crying?" he whispered.

"I don't know. I just feel so happy. I keep thinking about the girl I used to be and I wonder what would have happened if someone had told me then that I would end up here, with you. I wouldn't have believed it. I wouldn't have believed that my life could become this."

"Well you'd better believe it Sandi because it's happening," he said with a wide smile, kissing away my tears. We slipped away from each other, our bodies still singing to each other in this afterglow of love. The heat was uncomfortable, but we couldn't seem to let go of each other or keep our hands off each other. It was as though I would cease to exist if I was away from him for too long. He took my hand and kissed it.

"I'm never going to leave you Sandi."

"I'm never going to leave you Jack."

We linked hands as we made these solemn vows. I knew that more adventures were going to come, more vows would be made, but somehow these seemed to be the most important. We rose from the bed and walked to the shower, where we laughed at the scratch and bite marks we had left on each others' body in the throes of passion, the scars of love. We lathered each other and lost ourselves in the fine mist of the steamy water, embracing over and over again, for there was no end to our love. We wrapped each other up in soft towels and dried each other, cleansed and fresh before we returned to bed. I walked to the porch and let the cold air tease me. I looked out across the night sky, at this majestic place, and thought about how far I had come. I used to be a lonely girl with nothing but a dream in my heart. Over the years it had become harder to hold onto that dream, but Jack had infused my heart with hope again.

Now I knew that anything was possible. I had suffered enough in life. It was time for me to fly.

Jack walked up behind me and wrapped his arms around my waist. He bent down and kissed my neck, pulling away the wet strands of hair. I remarked how beautiful the night was, but he said that he only had eyes for me. I turned and kissed him again. The stars and the moon were the only witnesses to our love. We walked back inside the room. I blew out the candles one by one, and just as the last flame flickered out I slipped out of my gown and joined Jack in bed, finding his warm flesh in the smooth sheets. We giggled in the darkness, exploring our bodies once again as the world turned outside. The future beckoned us with all its majesty and all our plans of foundations and family and success, but that night was ours and ours alone. We held each other close as the world melted away. That night lasted an eternity, and I went to sleep with stars dancing in my eyes.

As I closed my eyes I thought about a time long ago, a time when I was sitting on a bench with the only friend I had in the world. We young and naïve, and knew nothing of the troubles life would bring us. He asked me what I wanted more than anything. I told him that I wanted to fall in love. At the time I thought my words were meant for him, but they weren't. I had been waiting for Jack to arrive, and once he did there was nothing stopping me from being with him. Everything else fell by the wayside and I spared a thought for the girl I had been, because I knew I was different now. She faded into the recesses of my mind. I whispered a goodbye, and she waved, gladly sacrificing herself for someone new, someone better, someone who had the confidence and the power to change people's lives.

I nestled my head against Jack's muscular chest and felt the steady beat of his heart underneath my ear. I closed my eyes and let myself fall asleep to that rhythm, while enjoying the warmth of his body. I thought of what the future might bring us. I thought of so many things, but most of all I thought of him. He soon fell asleep and he snored softly. I wondered if he would ever truly know how much I loved him. I kissed his chest and he murmured something in his sleep, before I let my head fall into the pillow and breathed heavily.

I let myself fall into slumber, eager for a new day to begin because it would be another one spent with the man of my dreams. Sometimes I went to sleep wondering what life would have been like had I not been given up by my parents, but on this occasion I didn't lament it. I had not lived an ordinary life, but the pain had been tempered by the sweet pleasure of falling in love with Jack.

*****

*****

Don't miss out!

Visit the website below and you can sign up to receive emails whenever Erica Frost publishes a new book. There's no charge and no obligation.

https://books2read.com/r/B-A-YRSV-HWTCC

BOOKS2READ

Connecting independent readers to independent writers.

Also by Erica Frost

Seduced By A Billionaire
Dark Secrets
A Billionaire's Game
Power Play
Ruthless Rival
Taming The Billionaire
The Hated Billionaire
3-Pointer